"You knew I'd follow you. Isn't that what you intended?"

Saul Kingsland certainly believed in the direct approach, Carly thought, rallying her defenses.

"You're a free agent, Mr. Kingsland."

"Not tonight." He shook his head. "I'm here to do a job—but I didn't know what I was looking for—what special qualities I needed—" He broke off, the cool eyes skimming over her, missing nothing.

Carly found the continuing silence unnerving. "And you know now?" she asked.

He said slowly, "Yes, I think I do. It's totally incredible." His gaze went down the curve of her body and it was as if he'd put out a hand and touched her intimately.

She thought, I don't know if I can go through with this. But I must....

SARA CRAVEN probably had the ideal upbringing for a budding writer. She grew up by the seaside in a house crammed with books, a box of old clothes to dress up in and a swing outside in a walled garden. She produced the opening of her first book at age five and is eternally grateful to her mother for having kept a straight face. Now she has more than twenty-five novels to her credit. The author is married and has two children.

Books by Sara Craven

HARLEQUIN PRESENTS

HARLEQUIN ROMANCE

Don't miss any of our special offers. Write to us at the following address for information on our newest releases.

Harlequin Reader Service
901 Fuhrmann Blvd., P.O. Box 1397, Buffalo, NY 14240
Canadian address: P.O. Box 603,
Fort Erie, Ont. L2A 5X3

SARA CRAVEN

flawless

Harlequin Books

TORONTO • NEW YORK • LONDON
AMSTERDAM • PARIS • SYDNEY • HAMBURG
STOCKHOLM • ATHENS • TOKYO • MILAN

Harlequin Presents first edition July 1990
ISBN 0-373-11279-3

Original hardcover edition published in 1989
by Mills & Boon Limited

CHAPTER ONE

'But you hate this kind of occasion,' said Clive. 'You always have. You call them "meat auctions" and "slave markets". You know you do.'

Carly, seated at her dressing-table, applying blusher with a practised hand, gave his irate reflection the smile the camera loved. 'That's quite right.'

'Then why in hell are we all going to the Flawless reception?'

'I changed my mind.'

'Now, that I don't believe.' Clive turned on his wife who was lounging on Carly's bed, leafing through a copy of *Harpers Bazaar*. 'Speak to her, Marge.'

'Waste of breath,' said Marge serenely. She eyed wistfully a photograph of a reed-slender black cocktail dress. 'Oh, why haven't I got thirty-four-inch hips?'

'Because you have three children,' said Clive, and brightened. 'Now there's a thought,' he said beguilingly. 'Why don't we scrap the Flawless do, go back to the house, and challenge the monsters to a team game of Trivial Pursuit?'

'No,' Marge and Carly said in unison, and he glared at them.

'Why not?'

'Because they always beat us,' said his wife.

'And because we're going to the Flawless party.' Carly reached for a mascara wand, and began to pay minute attention to her eyelashes. 'It's important to me, Clive.'

'Oh, for heaven's sake.' The end of Clive's tether seemed to be fast approaching. 'They want a pretty girl to launch a new range of cosmetics, that's all. Just because they've hyped it into the search for the new Scarlett O'Hara, it still doesn't make it any big deal.'

Carly sighed. 'Clive, you're my agent. Don't you want me to get work?'

'You do get work. I get you work. I have things in the pipeline now that will make the Flawless deal look like yesterday's news.' He dragged a chair forward and sat down. 'Sweetie, you're at a crucial point in your career. I don't think the Flawless job would be a particularly good move for you.'

'Is that what you've told all your clients?'

'Of course not,' he said. 'It will be a fabulous chance—for somebody.'

'Then why not me?'

'Because it would place you under an exclusive contract to them for a year and probably far longer. You wouldn't be able to take other assignments, and you'd be typed as the Flawless Girl for ever after.'

'I'm ready to risk that.'

'But why?' howled Clive. 'You've trusted my judgement in the past. Why are you doing this to me—to yourself?'

Carly replaced the mascara in her make-up kit. 'I have an instinct about it. Besides,' she paused, 'it's an ambition of mine to be photographed by Saul Kingsland.'

Marge looked up. 'Now you're talking,' she said. 'I hear he's an absolute dish. Good-looking and sexy as hell.'

'Oh, do you?' snorted Clive. 'Well, I hear he's a complete bastard. His models end up in tears, and his assistants have nervous breakdowns.'

Carly's brows rose. 'But he's a genius with a camera. And I suppose genius has to be allowed a certain amount of—artistic temperament.'

'That's not all Flawless are allowing him,' Clive said sourly. 'He also gets a free hand to pick The Girl.' He exhaled, frowning. 'Carly, every hopeful in modelling will be there tonight, parading themselves in front of him, and a few that should have given up hope by now,' he added grimly. 'You don't need to do this. If you're really so set on the damned job, I'll get on to Septimus Creed. His agency's handling the campaign, after all, so he should be able to pull some strings with Kingsland—and he owes me a favour...'

'No!' Carly banged her fist on the dressing-table, making the jars and bottles jump. Clive and Marge jumped too, and stared at her.

She bit her lip. 'I—I'm sorry. But I don't want any string-pulling. I want to go to the reception, and be chosen on my own merits.'

'And if you're not? It could be a pretty public rejection, sweetie. Everyone there will know you tried for it and failed.' Clive's face was sober.

'O, ye of little faith,' she said lightly.

'I'm serious. Supposing Saul Kingsland's idea of flawless is a five-foot blonde with baby-blue eyes, and a peaches-and-cream complexion?'

'That's your fantasy woman, darling, not Mr Kingsland's,' his wife said, getting to her feet. 'You've badgered Carly long enough. Now let's leave her to finish dressing in peace.' At the door, she paused. 'Have you ever actually met Saul Kingsland before, Carly?' she asked casually.

'Of course she hasn't met him,' Clive cut in impatiently. 'How could she have? She'd have still been a kid at school when he took off for America four years ago. And he hasn't been back since. I never thought he would come back.'

Marge shrugged. 'I only wondered,' she returned mildly, leading her still fuming husband into the sitting-room, and closing the door behind them.

Carly released a long, deep breath, letting sudden tension flow out of her.

'Take it easy,' she whispered to her mirrored image. 'You have a long night ahead of you.'

She eyed herself with a kind of clinical detachment, trying to see herself as Saul Kingsland would later that evening.

Her hair cascaded to her shoulders in wave after wave of burnished mahogany. Her eyes under the long sweep of mascaraed lashes were as cool and tranquil as aquamarines. She had a pale skin, a small, straight nose, a chin that was determined without being obtrusive, and a well-shaped mouth, the top lip clearly defined, the lower one curving in discreetly sensual promise.

'Flawless,' she said aloud, and with irony.

Her dress was aquamarine too, a simple, supple shape that left one shoulder bare, and she wore no jewellery, not even a watch.

I don't want to know when it's midnight. I might turn back into a pumpkin, she thought, and for a moment her hands clenched into fists at her sides.

But it couldn't happen. Here she was, after all, Carly North. One of modelling's newest and most successful faces. An up and coming name. Someone to be reckoned with in the cut-throat world of promoting beauty and fashion.

Just for a second, she wondered what the assignments were that Clive had been lining up for her, and allowed herself a brief pang of regret. Quite apart from the fact that he and Marge had become almost her second family, she had nothing but praise for the way he'd handled her career so far.

But she couldn't have second thoughts now. She'd waited too long for this chance. Her decision was made, and there was no going back.

She was going to be the Flawless Girl. She had to be.

She picked up her flask of First by Van Cleef and Arpels, and drew the glass stopper delicately over her pulse points. By the time she got to the reception, the fragrance would be blooming and alive on her skin.

Then she smiled at herself. It wasn't a smile that Marge, Clive, or the children would have recognised, or, indeed, any of the photographers she'd worked with in the past, who spoke of her warm vitality.

It was a harsh, almost feral twist of the lips.

'Saul Kingsland.' She said his name aloud like an incantation. 'You won't choose anyone else. You won't see anyone else.'

She picked up her wrap and went to join the others.

It was a warm night, and the long french windows of the hotel's banqueting suite had been thrown open. The balcony outside overlooked the hotel's sunken garden, a square of paved walks interleaving beds of crowding shrubs and roses.

Carly stood beside one of the open windows, and drew a deep, grateful breath. Clive had been so right about her loathing of this kind of party, she thought, grimacing inwardly. The clash of most of the popular scents on over-heated bodies vied for supremacy with the smell of alcohol, and the all-pervasive reek of tobacco smoke.

The champagne had been flowing freely all evening. Carly's own glass was almost untouched, but other people hadn't been so abstemious. Around her, voices were being raised, and laughter was a little too strident. Some of the other girls were looking flushed, too, and their immaculate grooming was becoming frayed round the edges.

If he keeps us all waiting much longer, people will start passing out, Carly told herself. But perhaps that's how he's going to make his choice— the only girl still vertical at the end of the evening.

Her mouth curled in distaste at the thought. In fact, Saul Kingsland's delayed appearance at the reception spoke of arrogance of the worst kind. But maybe the man who was being spoken of, since his recent return from the States, as the natural successor to David Bailey and Patrick Lichfield, felt himself above the consideration of other people's feelings or convenience. If so, he would undoubtedly be a swine to work with.

Good, Carly thought, lifting her hair away from the nape of her neck for a moment so that the faint breeze could caress her skin. That suits me just fine.

'Carly, I thought it was you.' Gina Lesley, with whom she'd worked on a bathing-suit feature in the Bahamas, appeared from nowhere. 'Isn't this whole thing unbelievable? It's like being in some harem, and waiting for the Sultan to appear and pick one of us for the night.'

'They say it's exactly like that,' an elfin-faced girl, her red hair exotically tipped with gold, broke in eagerly. 'Lauren reckons that Saul Kingsland sleeps with all his models. Do you suppose it's true?'

Gina gave Carly a speaking look. 'I shouldn't think so for a moment,' she returned crushingly. 'If he went in for that kind of bedroom athletics he wouldn't be able to focus his eyes, let alone a camera.'

The other girl pouted and walked off.

'Incredible,' Gina muttered. 'In fact, the latest whisper from the powder-room says that we're all wasting our time because the great man has no intention of showing here tonight.'

Carly was very still. 'I hope that isn't true,' she said sharply.

'So do I, darling. And to add to my depression, one of the hacks from the Creed agency is spreading the word that Saul Kingsland is going for a total unknown—someone he'll see in the street, or serving in a shop, maybe.'

'I don't believe it,' Carly said. 'They wouldn't be throwing away their money on a bash like this if that was the case.'

Gina grinned at her. 'Positive thinking,' she said. 'That's what I like to hear.' She paused. 'Oddly enough, you were the last person I expected to see here tonight.'

Carly shrugged. 'I have to eat, too,' she returned. 'I just wish it was all over, and we could go home.'

'Well, something seems to be happening at last.' Gina craned her neck. 'Some of the Flawless bigwigs are milling about, and Septimus Creed is doing his marshalling act. I think someone's going to make a speech.'

The chairman of the company producing the new cosmetic range mounted the flower-decked dais at the end of the room, and tested the microphone a shade uncertainly. After the usual words of welcome, he launched into an enthusiastic description of the new range.

'Flawless,' he told them, 'is not just another brand of make-up. We regard it as a total look— part of today's woman's complete way of life— hypo-allergenic, yet highly fashion-conscious at the same time. And we pride ourselves on the fact that we are leading the way in banning animal testing from our laboratories.'

Carly joined in the dutiful ripple of applause, and took a sideways step towards the open window to gulp another breath of fresh air. And in that moment she saw him.

He was standing at the head of the short flight of stairs which led down into the banqueting suite from its main entrance, his eyes restlessly scanning the crowded room.

He was tall, she thought, her gaze devouring him. Broad-shouldered and lean-hipped. He was by no means conventionally handsome. His features were too strong—too assertive with those heavy-lidded grey eyes, jutting chin, and a nose that was almost a beak. He shouldn't even have been attractive, Carly told herself. His face was too thin, and the lines round his face and mouth altogether too cynical. His hair was too long, and the formality of his dinner-jacket sat uneasily on him, Carly told herself critically. His tie was slightly crooked, as if he'd wrenched at its constriction with an impatient hand.

Yet in spite of this—because of this?—he was attractive. Devastatingly, heart-stoppingly, un-equivocally attractive. All man, someone had called him once, and it was true. A man who spent his life among beautiful women, and enjoyed that life to the full.

But no one else had noticed his arrival, Carly realised as she stared across at him. They were all facing the dais, listening to the chairman's peroration.

With total deliberation and concentration, she focused all her attention on him, willing him to turn his head, and see her.

Look at me, she commanded silently. Look at me now.

Slowly, as if she was operating some invisible magnet, Saul Kingsland's head turned, and across the room their eyes met.

For a long moment Carly held his gaze, then she deliberately snapped the thread, turning to watch Septimus Creed who'd followed the chairman on to the dais and was outlining the thinking behind the plans for the campaign.

'The Flawless concept is one of total freshness—naturalness—even purity,' he was saying. 'And this is what we want our Flawless Girl to represent.'

'Well, that cuts me out,' Gina whispered with a humorous grimace.

Carly forced a smile in return, but said nothing. Her mind was working feverishly. She'd made him notice her, but was it—would it be enough?

It means so much, she thought. It has to be enough. Has to.

'My goodness!' Gina's eyes were widening. 'Do you see who's here—who's actually arrived? How long do you think he's been standing there?' She took a breath. 'I'm going over to say hello. Introduce myself. Coming with me?'

Carly shook her head. 'I'll catch up with you later, Gina. I—I need some air.'

It wasn't an excuse. The force of her emotions was making her feel dizzy. She slipped out on to the balcony, and stood leaning on the stone balustrade looking down into the garden. Lamps had been lit now among the tall shrubs, and the scent of the roses was warm and strong in the evening air. Above the bulk of the hotel building, a crescent moon hung like a slash of gold in the sapphire sky.

Carly looked up at the moon, and inclined her head to it, as the old superstition dictated.

'Oh, moon,' she whispered silently. 'I wish—oh, how I wish...'

'Good evening.' The sound of his voice from the doorway behind her made Carly start violently. She spun to face him, the fragile wine-glass falling from her hand to shatter on the tiles at her feet.

'Are you all right?' Two long strides brought him to her side. 'You haven't cut yourself?'

'No,' she forced from her taut throat. 'I—it's just some champagne on my dress.'

'Damnation.' He produced an immaculate handkerchief. 'Let me see...'

She took a step backwards. 'I can manage—really.'

He'd followed her, and that was incredible. But it was also too soon. He'd caught her off guard. She wasn't ready for this confrontation—and she certainly wasn't ready to be touched by him.

'Just as you wish.' He sounded faintly surprised, but he passed her the handkerchief, and she dabbed at her dress, her hands shaking, sharply aware that he was watching her.

He said abruptly, 'You're very nervous.'

'What do you expect? You—startled me.'

'I shouldn't have sneaked up on you like that.' Saul Kingsland's smile contained both repentance and charm. He paused. 'But then, you knew I'd follow you—didn't you? Isn't that exactly what you intended?'

He certainly believed in the direct approach, Carly thought, rallying her defences.

'You're a free agent, Mr Kingsland.'

He shook his head. 'Not tonight. I'm here to do a job—fulfil an obligation. I have to find a face—a body around which an entire advertising campaign can pivot. Frankly, I thought it was impossible—a gimmick foisted on me by Septimus Creed. How could I choose anyone when I didn't know what I was looking for—what special qualities I needed?' He broke off, the cool eyes skimming over her, missing nothing.

Carly found the intensity of his scrutiny and the continuing silence unnerving. She broke it deliberately, moving backwards, resting an elbow on the balustrade. 'And do you know now?'

He said slowly, 'Yes, I think I do. It's totally incredible.'

His gaze went down the curve of her body as she lounged against the stonework, lingering on breast and thigh. It was as if he'd put out a hand and touched her intimately, and she was hard put to it not to flinch.

She thought, I don't know if I can go through with this. But I must . . .

She laughed. 'Is this your usual line, Mr Kingsland? "Put yourself in my hands, little girl, and I'll make you famous"?' She pulled a face. 'A little tacky, don't you think?'

'Yes—if it were true.' He sounded impatient. 'But I assure you I'm not just shooting a line. I should know your name. Why don't I? Who's your agent?'

'My name is Carly North,' she said. 'My agent is Clive Monroe, and if you're not careful, I shall begin to think you mean this.'

'Believe it,' he said shortly. His brows drew together in a frown. 'Or is there some problem?'

She shrugged. 'Perhaps I'm not sure I want to be the Flawless Girl.'

'Then what are you doing here?'

'Natural curiosity. Normally I avoid this kind of situation like the plague.'

'Then we have something in common at least.' He gave her a long, speculative look. 'So, I have to persuade you, do I?'

'Not easy,' she said, lightly. 'I have a mind of my own, and my career is going well. Ask Clive.'

'I intend to. But that doesn't let you off the hook.' He paused. 'I have to stay at this thing for a while, but will you have dinner with me when it's over?'

'With my agent?'

'If necessary.'

'He's a family man. He might not be able to make it.'

'All the better.'

'You don't waste any time.'

'Why should I? The deadlines have been drawn—quite apart from any personal considerations.'

Carly's brows lifted. 'You seem to be living up to your reputation.'

'I don't have a reputation,' he said. 'These days, I'm a stranger in town.'

'Hardly,' she said. 'There can't be a person in the country who hasn't heard of you.'

'Professionally, maybe. On other levels, they know nothing, and nor do you. So, ignore rumour and hearsay. Use your own instincts—your own judgement about me, Carly North.'

'Perhaps my instincts are warning me to run.'

'Then they're playing you false,' he said slowly. 'Besides, if that were true, why did you want me to notice you so badly just now?'

'Is that what I did?' Alarm tingled on her skin.

'You know it is. And if it wasn't for strictly professional reasons, then it must have had a personal basis.'

She said coolly, 'That's a rather arrogant assumption.'

Saul Kingsland shrugged. 'Then that could be something else we have in common.'

'What do you mean?'

'Isn't it a form of arrogance to come here tonight, looking as you do, when you don't really want the Flawless job?'

'I didn't say that,' she said quickly. 'I said I wasn't sure.'

'So, I'm asking again, will you have dinner with me later, and let me convince you?'

She felt as if she was being swept along, caught in a current she couldn't control. A voice in her head was screaming at her to refuse, warning her frantically that this was all too much, too soon.

She said, 'Very well.' She shot him a veiled look. 'But I'm promising nothing.'

'Professionally?' Saul Kingsland asked silkily. 'Or personally?'

'Both.'

'Fine,' he said equably. 'Then we know where we stand.' He smiled at her. 'And now I'd better justify my presence here—mix a little—talk to some people.' He paused. 'Don't run away.'

'I gave that up,' she said, 'a long time ago.'

She watched him walk away, back into the lighted room. Leaving her alone.

Relief flooded through her, making her feel almost light-headed. She sagged against the balustrade, her legs trembling, staring sightlessly in front of her as her mind revolved over and over again everything that had happened, everything that had been said between them.

In the end, it had been easy. Too easy, perhaps. Certainly not what she'd expected.

What have I done? she thought, a pang of unease shivering through her. What have I started? I've got a tiger by the tail, and I can't—I dare not let go.

There was no turning back, not now. And perhaps there never was.

Squaring her shoulders, she went to find Clive.

CHAPTER TWO

SAUL KINGSLAND'S car was long, sleek and powerful. Of course, Carly thought, her lip curling as she settled herself into the passenger seat.

Their departure from the reception together had caused something of a sensation. The atmosphere of disappointment and frustration among the other girls had been almost tangible.

'I just hope you know what you're doing, that's all,' had been Clive's valediction.

And Marge had said softly, 'Oh, I'm sure she does.'

I shall have to be careful with Marge, Carly thought, as Saul eased the car into the traffic. She's altogether too shrewd.

'Do you like Italian food?' Saul asked. 'Or are you on some kind of permanent diet?'

'Good lord, no.' She gave a slight shrug. 'I suppose I'm lucky. I seem to burn up a lot of calories.'

'Yes, I can believe that. You're very cool on the surface, but underneath I suspect there's a mass of tension.'

She bit her lip. 'Not that I'm aware of.' She gave him a small cool smile. 'I'm a very uncomplicated person, actually.'

'I'll let you know about that,' he said, 'when we're better acquainted.'

'Comments like that make me nervous,' she replied. 'I like my privacy.'

'But if we're going to work together—achieve some kind of rapport, we can't remain strangers.'

'You think it's all decided, don't you? All sewn up.' There was an edge to her voice.

'I'm taking nothing for granted where you're concerned, lady. That's why we're having this meal together—to see if we can establish some kind of basis to proceed from.'

'And if we can't?'

It was Saul's turn to shrug. 'Then I find another Flawless Girl from somewhere. No one's irreplaceable, after all.'

'Is that Public Warning Number One?'

'You're in the business,' he said. 'You know the score as well as I do.' There was a brief silence, then, 'Your agent really doesn't want you to do this, does he?'

'Clive has—reservations.'

'But he said it was your decision.' He sent her a sideways glance. 'He made me wonder if you were just playing games with me—playing hard to get.'

'Of course not. Why on earth should I?' Her mouth was dry suddenly.

'You tell me,' he said laconically.

Carly was quiet for a moment. Then she said, 'Perhaps I should put my cards on the table. I was in two minds about the Flawless assignment when I went to the reception tonight. I—I still am, come to that.' She ran the tip of her tongue along her lower lip. 'But you were right about one thing—I did want you to notice me, and that was even before I realised who you were.'

'I'm flattered.'

'And I'm ashamed,' she returned. 'I shocked myself this evening. I don't usually—come on so strong.' She forced a little laugh. 'There—confession over.'

'You won't be made to do penance,' he said. 'I'm glad to know the attraction was mutual. Now, all we have to do is relax and enjoy the rest of the evening.'

He found a parking space, and they walked the remaining hundred yards to the restaurant's entrance. Carly had half expected Saul to put his hand under her arm, or clasp her fingers with his as they walked along, but he made no attempt to touch her even in a casual way. In view of her recent admission, she found this restraint intriguing, but she was relieved by it too.

It wasn't a large restaurant, and it relied heavily on the intimacy of its atmosphere. The lights were low, the tables screened from each other by trellis-work covered in climbing plants, and in one corner a lone guitarist played music which was pleasant without being obtrusive.

'The food here used to be wonderful,' Saul remarked, handing her a menu.

It still was. They ate stuffed courgette flowers, and scallops grilled in their shells, followed by *osso buco* and roast quails with *polenta*. To finish the meal Carly had a frothy chocolate concoction, rich with cream and liqueur, and Saul asked for cheese. The coffee was strong, black and aromatic, and served with Strega.

While they ate, the conversation had been general. Carly had encouraged Saul to talk about his life in America, and the glossy magazine scene in New York. He also told her about a book he had coming out.

'I did a hell of a lot of travelling while I was over there,' he said. 'So, it's a kind of odyssey in pictures. My tribute to everything I liked best about life Stateside. Places and people that I loved.'

His tone gave nothing away, but Carly found herself wondering how many of those people had been women.

'It sounds—illuminating,' she said. 'Do you intend to go back to America?'

Saul signalled for more coffee. 'At the moment, I'm not sure,' he said. 'My plans are—fluid. I need to see how things work out for me here, once the Flawless assignment is finished.' He paused. 'And, while we're on the subject, have you come to any decision yet?'

Carly gasped. 'I've hardly had time to think,' she began.

'Really?' He gave her a straight look. 'I had the impression several times tonight that you were so deep in thought you were a million miles away.'

She flushed a little. 'I'm sorry if I've been poor company...'

'I didn't say that.' He leaned forward. 'If you're still not sure, spend the day with me tomorrow, and I'll take some pictures of you—convince you that way.'

Carly shook her head. 'I can't tomorrow. I'm going home to visit.'

'Where is home?'

'In the country. Very quiet and dull.'

'With you there?' He slanted a smile at her. 'Impossible. Tell you what, why don't I come with you? I was going to walk you along the Embankment and through the parks, but a rural background would be even better.'

'I'm sorry, but it's out of the question.' Her flush deepened. 'It's going to be rather hectic—a houseful of people. My sister's getting engaged.'

'Not so quiet and dull, after all,' he said.

'It usually is. My family is—very conventional. I don't think they altogether approve of my life in London.'

'And what heinous sins do they think you commit? Perhaps I could reassure them.'

'But you don't know me,' she said. 'You don't know what I'm capable of.'

'Not at this moment,' he said. 'But I intend to know you, Carly North, in every way there is.'

He was smiling, but as the grey eyes met hers Carly was conscious of a curious intentness in their depths. She felt vulnerable suddenly, and afraid, as if Saul's gaze was probing too deeply, staring straight into her mind, laying bare all her innermost secrets.

Her heart missed a beat, and her throat felt tight. She said huskily, 'I find remarks like that— distasteful.'

'Then I apologise.' He didn't sound sorry at all. 'I'll begin our acquaintance solely through the lens of a camera, and in no other way, I swear.' He stretched out a hand to her across the table, and reluctantly she allowed his fingers to close round hers. 'Will you work with me, Carly North? Will you be my Flawless Girl?'

'I can't tell you now. I have to think about it.'
She withdrew her hand from his grasp. 'May I have
the weekend?'

'I won't argue with that.' He took a diary out of
an inside pocket of his dinner-jacket, tore out a page
and scribbled down a telephone number. 'Call me
on this when you've decided.' He paused. 'You say
that your sister's getting engaged. What about you,
Carly? You're not wearing any rings, but that
doesn't mean a whole lot in these liberated days.
Are you attached? Are there any lovers or hus-
bands lurking in your vicinity?'

'There's nobody.'

'You astound me.'

'It's through my own choice.' She despised the
defensiveness in her own voice.

'I'm sure it is.'

'Am I allowed to ask you the same question?
How many ex-wives have you left sighing over you?'

'None at all—and no present Mrs Kingsland
either.' He was laughing openly. 'I am entirely
without encumbrances.'

Of course he was, she thought. Saul Kingsland
was a rolling stone, a man who would never settle
or opt for an ordered existence. He would walk into
a woman's life, take what he wanted, and walk on
without a backward look. A wreaker of havoc,
unknowing and uncaring. And you didn't even have
to be a woman to suffer at his hands.

Abruptly, Carly pushed back her chair. 'I really
should be going.'

'Already? It's still relatively early.'

'I have to leave first thing in the morning. My
mother will be needing help with the arrangements.'

'Ah, yes,' he said softly. 'The devoted daughter rushing back to the bosom of the family. Oddly enough, that's not the impression I had of you. When I saw you standing in the moonlight, I thought I'd never seen anyone look so solitary—so used to being alone. It just shows how wrong one can be.'

'First impressions are often misleading.' She made her voice deliberately dismissive. 'Would you ask someone to find me a cab, please?'

Saul looked at her in surprise. 'There's no need for that. I'll drive you home.'

'I—I don't want to take you out of your way.'

'That's very thoughtful of you.' His smile was sardonic. 'How do you know that you will be?'

'I—don't, actually.'

'Then there's no more to be said,' he told her, indicating to the head waiter that he required the bill.

Carly bit her lip, trying to hide her annoyance.

'Do you never take "no" for an answer?' she enquired acidly, when they were in the car, and he was following her reluctantly given instructions.

'It depends on how positive the "no" is,' he said. 'In your case it was just a ploy to prevent me knowing where you lived for some reason, and a useless ploy at that.'

'Why do you say that?'

'Because there are plenty of ways of finding your address if I were sufficiently desperate,' he said. 'There's the phone book, for starters.' He slanted a frowning look at her. 'So, for goodness' sake calm down, and stop being so damned uptight,' he went on. 'There's nothing to be scared of. You have my word on that. I'm not going to pressure you, or make a nuisance of myself by camping on your doorstep. Perhaps events have moved rather too fast tonight, but from now on we'll take things just as easily as you wish.'

'Thank you.' Her hands gripped tautly together in her lap.

'I learned some relaxation techniques in the States.' He didn't miss a thing. He added, with a smile in his voice, 'If you asked me nicely, I might be prepared to teach them to you.'

'I'll bear it in mind.' She made herself speak lightly. She'd let him think she'd been instantly attracted to him, for heaven's sake. Now she was treating him as if he was some plague carrier. 'Actually, you're quite right. This evening has been— totally outside my experience. I'm in a state of complete confusion.'

'I'm still in shock myself,' Saul said drily. 'Perhaps the weekend will help us get our heads together.'

The remainder of the journey was completed in silence, to Carly's relief.

Saul stopped the car, and glanced up at the block of flats. 'Very nice,' he commented. 'Your career really is doing well.' He paused. 'Do you live by yourself?'

She shook her head. 'I share with another girl. She works for a television company.'

'Is she there at the moment?'

'No,' Carly said, before she could stop herself. 'She's abroad with a film crew.'

'Then I'll go up with you,' he said.

She looked at him in total dismay, and his mouth tightened.

'And not for the reasons you seem to think,' he added bitingly. 'My motives are actually quite chivalrous. I want to make sure you get home safely.'

'Don't you feel you're being rather over-protective?'

'No, I don't. I took a girl home from a party in New York over a year ago. She was independent, too, and insisted on saying goodnight on the pavement. When she got up to her apartment, someone had broken in, and she was attacked and badly injured. If I'd insisted on escorting her to the door, it might not have happened. I'm not taking the risk again.'

'In case you hadn't noticed, this is London, not New York.'

'Just a different part of the jungle, lady.' He walked up the steps beside her, and opened the swing doors.

She stood beside him in the lift in resentful silence. Walked along the passage to the door, still without speaking.

"May I have your key?" Saul held out his hand.

'Oh, this is silly,' Carly burst out in exasperation as she gave it to him. 'Just how many times do you think I've come back here alone at night? Lucy's away a lot.'

'That was in the bad old days.' He unlocked the door, and pushed it open. 'Now you don't have to be alone any more, unless you want to be.'

Carly lifted her chin. 'Is that a hint that you want to stay for more coffee—or a nightcap—or whatever the current euphemism is? How very obvious.'

'No,' he said calmly. 'It's more a declaration of intent.'

He was standing very close to her. She could actually feel the warmth of his body. Suddenly Carly found it difficult to breathe. Any moment now, she thought wildly, and he would reach out for her, take her in his arms, and she was terrified. She felt as if she was balanced on a knife-edge, every nerve-ending tingling in alarm and anticipation.

Kiss me, she thought, her heart beating violently against her ribcage. Kiss me and get it over with.

As he moved, her eyelids fluttered down, and her lips parted in a little unconscious sigh. Her whole body tensed, waiting to feel his hands on her, his mouth against hers.

He said quietly, 'Goodnight, Flawless Girl. Call me after the weekend, and let me know what you've decided.'

The door closed softly, and he was gone.

Carly's eyes flew open, and she stood rigid for a long moment, staring at the enigmatic wooden panels; then, with a small sob, she hurled herself forward, putting up the chain and securing the interior bolt with hands that shook.

She'd been so sure that, in spite of her protestations, he would offer at least a token pass. Now, paradoxically, she felt that he'd made a fool of her.

And that's ridiculous, she thought. Because Saul Kingsland is the one who's been fooled. I've done it. I've succeeded. I've won.

She laughed out loud, and the sound echoed eerily in the quiet flat.

She walked into her bedroom, shedding her few clothes as she went, and straight into the bathroom which separated her room from Lucy's, stepping into the shower, and turning the warm spray full on. She stood motionless, letting the water pour over her, soaking her hair, and running in rivulets down her skin.

Washing Saul Kingsland away.

But only for the time being, she reminded herself with a sharp stab of excitement as she reluctantly turned off the water, and stepped back on to the thick mat, reaching for a towel.

On Monday, she would make that call, and after that—she drew a breath. After that, whatever would be, would be.

As she turned, she caught a glimpse of herself in the mirror, and almost recoiled. It was like seeing a stranger, or her own bad angel, eyes glittering with malevolence, bright, febrile colour along her cheekbones, the soft mouth starkly compressed.

Revenge might be sweet, but, dear heaven, what would it cost her in human terms?

The image in the mirror blurred suddenly and, bending her head, Carly began to weep—for the girl she'd been, and for the woman she'd become.

The sun was pouring into the bedroom the next morning, as she packed a weekend bag with her usual economy. The dress she had bought specially to wear for the party was already waiting in its protective cover, and she grimaced slightly as she lifted it down and carried it out to her car.

A greater contrast to the dress she'd worn the previous night could not be imagined, she thought wryly. But then, she hardly looked the same girl at all. She was simply and casually dressed in tailored cream linen trousers with a matching jacket over a short-sleeved khaki T-shirt. Her hair was gathered into a single plait, and allowed to hang over one shoulder, and her face was innocent of all cosmetics but a touch of moisturiser.

As she loaded the car, she couldn't resist a furtive look round. In spite of his assurances, Saul Kingsland might be there watching her, perhaps from one of the row of parked cars across the street.

Oh, stop it, she adjured herself impatiently. That's the way to paranoia.

Traffic was heavy, and getting out of London required all her concentration. She couldn't relax until trees and fields began to replace suburban sprawl. She lowered the window a little, to enjoy the sunlit breeze, and put a cassette of Vivaldi's *Four Seasons* into the tape machine, then sat back to savour the remainder of her journey.

An hour later, she turned the car into the gravelled sweep of the drive and saw the familiar redbrick Georgian bulk of the house awaiting her. She drove round to the rear, and parked in the former stables, slotting her Polo in between her father's Bentley and the sedate estate car her mother preferred.

She sat for a moment, staring in front of her, then, with a smothered sigh, collected her things, and walked down the covered way to the side entrance.

There was a lot of activity already, she saw. A large marquee had been erected on the lawn, and folding tables and chairs were being carried into it. As she watched, a florist's van drew up in front of the house, and two women dressed in pink overalls got out. Presently, no doubt, the caterers' vehicles would also be arriving.

Mother will be in her element, Carly thought, her mouth twisting. She'll be able to use it as a trial run for Susan's actual wedding. And I'm about as necessary in all this as an extra thumb.

She caught a movement in the large conservatory which flanked the lawn and, smiling a little, trod quietly across the gravel and stood in the doorway watching the tall, grey-haired man who was deftly repotting some plants.

'Hello, Father.'

He turned with an obvious start, and peered at her. 'Why, Caroline,' he said, 'so you've come. Your mother wasn't sure... Well, this is splendid—splendid.' He paused, then added another vague, 'Splendid.'

Carly bit her lip. 'I did say I was coming,' she said, quietly. 'If I'm not expected—if my room's being used, I can always try the pub.'

'Certainly not. I'm sure your room's ready and waiting for you, my dear, although, of course, your mother always handles those arrangements. She's in the drawing-room, having coffee with your Aunt Grace. I said I'd join them once I'd finished this and washed my hands, but now...' His voice tailed off expectantly.

'But now that I've arrived, it will let you off the hook,' Carly supplied drily.

'Well, all this talk about engagements and weddings,' he said. 'Not my sort of thing at all, you know. They'll start on christenings next, I dare say,' he added with disfavour.

'I can imagine.' Carly slanted a smile at him. 'Stay with your beloved plants, Dad. I'll try and ensure you're not missed.'

As she entered the hall, she could hear Aunt Grace's authoritative tones issuing from the drawing-room. She pulled a small face. Her mother's older sister held strong views on everything, from the government in power down to the deplorable attitude of today's shop assistants. Since her only daughter's marriage and departure for New Zealand a few years previously, she had lived in Bournemouth, which she rarely left. Carly couldn't help wishing that she had not decided to make an exception to this excellent rule for Susan's engagement party.

She resolutely pinned on a smile as she went into the drawing-room. 'Hello, Mummy, Aunt Grace. How are you both?'

There was an immediate surprised silence. Carly was aware of both pairs of eyes riveted on her, taking in every detail of her appearance. She put down her case, and draped her dress-carrier over the back of a chair.

'Is that coffee? I'd love some.'

'Of course, dear.' Mrs Foxcroft filled the third cup waiting on the tray and proffered it to her younger daughter. 'Did you have a good drive down?'

'Marvellous, thank you.' Carly bent and kissed her mother's cheek, and, more fleetingly, her aunt's. 'You're both looking very well.'

Her mother smiled awkwardly. 'And so are you, darling. Positively—radiant. Isn't she, Grace?'

'Hm,' said Mrs Brotherton. 'Try as I may, Veronica, I still cannot accustom myself... However,' she turned to Carly, 'I saw a photograph of you in a magazine at my hairdressers' last month, Caroline. You were wearing an extraordinary garment in white taffeta, and seemed to be standing in an area of slum clearance.'

'Oh, the Fabioni. I remember it well.' Carly laughed. 'It was incredibly cold that day—the middle of winter, in fact—and we were down by the river. Did you manage to count my goose-pimples?'

'I find it very odd,' said Aunt Grace majestically, 'that a reputable journal should find it necessary to photograph an evening dress outdoors in broad daylight, and inclement weather.'

'It's because of publishing schedules,' Carly told her. 'Fur coats in August, and bikinis in December. The bane of a model's life.' She looked at her mother. 'Where's Susan? Resting for the big occasion?'

'She's gone with Anthony to look at the house his father is giving them as a wedding present. Apparently it needs a great deal doing to it, and work will have to start almost at once if it's to be ready for them to move into after the wedding.'

'Have they set a date yet?' Carly asked casually. 'I'll need to know fairly well in advance.'

'I believe they're thinking of October,' her mother returned. 'I know Susan wants to talk to you about it,' she added, after a pause.

'Oh, good.' Carly drank some of her coffee, feeling another silence about to press down on them all. She decided to prevent it. 'How are James and Louise?' she asked her aunt.

'They seem happily settled. The farm is not too isolated, fortunately, so Louise can get into the nearby town for shopping, and other essentials. She is expecting another baby in July.'

'So soon?' That made three in just over five years, Carly thought, blinking. 'Maybe Louise should consider spending even more time in town,' she joked feebly.

'Caroline, dear,' her mother said repressively, while Aunt Grace looked more forbidding than ever.

'I'm sorry.' Carly drained her cup, and rose to her feet. 'I'll go and unpack. Am I in my old room?'

'Well, actually, dear, I was wondering if you'd mind using the nursery—just this once, of course. Jean and Arthur Lewis found they could come, after all, and as it's such a long way for them to travel I did offer...'

'...my room to them.' Carly completed the hesitant sentence. 'Of course they must have it. They're such old friends, after all. I quite understand. Well—I'll see you both later.' She paused at the door. 'If there's anything I can do to help, you only have to ask.'

'That's very sweet of you, dear, but everything's under control.'

'Yes,' Carly said gently, 'I'm sure it is.'

Susan's engagement to Anthony Farrar, the son of a local landowner, had been hoped for and planned for over a very long period, she thought with irony as she climbed the broad sweep of stairs. Susan had first met Anthony at a hunt ball when she was eighteen, and had made up her mind there and then to marry him. Everything that had happened since had been like a long and fraught military campaign, with triumphs and reverses in almost equal proportions.

Carly herself had wondered more than once if Anthony was worth all this agonising over. He was attractive enough in a fair-haired, typically English way—certainly better-looking than either of his sisters, she allowed judiciously—but she'd always found him humourless, and suspected as well that he might share his father's notoriously roving eye.

But Susan clearly regarded her engagement as a major victory, Carly thought wryly, as she went up the second flight of stairs to the old nursery quarters. So, heaven forbid that she should be a dissenting voice amid the jubilation.

Not that Sue would listen if I was, she thought with a sigh, as she opened the nursery door.

It was hardly recognisable as the room she and her sister had once shared. All the old furniture had gone, and so had the toys—the doll's house, the rocking-horse, and the farmyard animals. It was now, very obviously, a very spare bedroom, she thought, dumping her case down on the narrow single bed, furnished with unwanted odds and ends from the rest of the house. Only the white-painted bars across the windows revealed its original purpose.

She opened her case and put the few items it contained into the chest of drawers.

The photograph, as always, was at the bottom of the case. She extracted it, and placed it carefully on the dressing-chest next to the mirror.

She stood for a long moment, staring at it. The child's face looked back at her, its eager brightness diminished by the heavy glasses, and the protruding front teeth that the shy smile revealed.

Slowly, her hands curled into taut fists at her sides, and as gradually relaxed again.

An object lesson in how not to look.

And one, she thought, that she would never forget.

CHAPTER THREE

CARLY adjusted the neckline of her dress, and gave it a long, disparaging look. As a garment, she supposed it was adequate. The material was good—a fine, silky crêpe—and it had been competently put together. But the Puritan grey did nothing for her, and with her hair twisted up into a smooth topknot she looked bland and unobtrusive, like a Victorian governess.

But that, of course, was precisely her intention.

It had been a long afternoon. She'd made another diffident offer of help downstairs which had been kindly but firmly refused. Instead she'd found herself being subjected to an exhaustive commentary on the problems of sheep farming in New Zealand by Aunt Grace.

In the end she'd taken refuge in a sunny corner of the garden, so far untouched by the demands of the party, with an armful of books from her childhood which she'd rescued from the attic. It had been wonderful to discover that *The House at Pooh Corner* had lost none of its old magic and step once more into *Tom's Midnight Garden*. She found a new serenity burgeoning within her as she relaxed with them.

Over tea in the drawing-room she'd looked at the multitude of snapshots Aunt Grace had triumphantly produced of James, Louise and the children, and said all the right things. Or she hoped she had.

James looked flourishing, tanned and handsome. The kind of man who'd be an achiever whatever he set his hand to. But Louise, she thought privately, looked weary, her radiant blonde prettiness muted somehow, as if the everyday demands of babies and farming were becoming too much for her.

But then Louise had always enjoyed the urban life—London with its buzz, its theatres and parties. For her, the country had been somewhere to spend the occasional weekend. Strange then that she should have married James, and accepted the radical change of life-style he was offering, rather than one of his wealthy and sophisticated friends.

Of course, Louise might consider that the world she was used to was well lost for love, but Carly didn't think so. Not on the evidence of these photographs, anyway.

As soon as she could, she escaped upstairs again, and had a lingering, scented bath, mindful of her mother's adjuration to vacate the bathroom in good time, ready for Susan's use.

'It is her night, after all, dear.'

Carly felt that the reminder was unnecessary. She was conscious too of a nagging disappointment that Susan's house-viewing trip was taking so long. It had been ages since she'd seen her sister—talked to her. In fact, it was Christmas, she realised. Each time she'd been home briefly since, Susan had been preoccupied with Anthony.

She took one last look at herself, and turned away from the mirror, glancing at her watch. Well, Sue

was bound to have returned by now. She could go
down to her room and chat to her while she got
ready, as they'd done when they were younger.

She went down the short flight of stairs, and
walked along the passage. As she lifted a hand to
tap at the door, it occurred to her that once she
would simply have barged cheerfully in.

'Come in,' Sue called, and Carly turned the
handle and walked into the room.

Sue swung round on her dressing-stool. 'Oh, it's
you.' Her smile was perfunctory. 'How are you,
Caro?'

'I'm fine.' Carly deposited herself on the bed.
'You don't mind if I stay—talk to you while you
dress?'

Sue shrugged. 'If you want. But I don't have a
lot of time to spare. I stayed longer than I should
have done with Anthony's mother, talking about
the wedding.'

'Oh.' Carly hesitated for a moment. 'Would you
like me to do your make-up for you?'

'No, thank you.' Sue's voice had an edge to it.
'I may not have the professional touch, but I've
managed adequately up to now. Besides, Anthony
prefers me to look natural.'

Carly felt herself flush. 'I—wasn't criticising. I
thought it might relax you.'

'I'm perfectly relaxed,' Sue said shortly, reaching
for the moisturiser.

Carly bit her lip. 'I can always go away, if you
prefer.'

'No, you may as well stay. I've been wanting to
talk to you anyway about arrangements for the
wedding.' She fidgeted for a moment with the lid

of the jar, then burst out, 'Caro, would you mind awfully if you weren't a bridesmaid?'

Carly stared at her, feeling as if she'd been pole-axed. She said slowly, 'Not a bridesmaid? But Sue, we promised each other ever since we were little . . . Of course I'd mind.'

'Yes, I know that.' Sue's tone was impatient, dismissive. 'But things change—circumstances alter. And I've decided to have just Anthony's sisters instead. They're both shorter than you, and blonde. It would be practically impossible to find a colour you all could wear, and next to them you'd look like a giraffe anyway.'

'I—see.' Hurt and disappointment were warring inside Carly with a growing anger. 'It didn't occur to you to have me alone?'

'No, it didn't, frankly.'

'Even though I'm your only sister?'

Bright spots of colour burned in Sue's cheeks. 'Listen,' she said, 'whether you like it or not, I only intend to get married once, and it's going to be my big day, from beginning to end. I'm not prepared to be—outshone by anyone. I want them all to be looking at me as I walk up the aisle, not at whoever's following me.'

'You think I wouldn't take a back seat—that I'd push for attention?' Carly spread her hands. 'Sue, I wouldn't—I swear it.'

'You couldn't help it. If you walked around with a bag over your head, people would still look at you. It's the way you hold yourself—the way you move—everything.' Sue slammed down the jar. 'Anyway, there's no use in arguing about it. My mind's made up. I've already spoken to Tess and

Sarah.' She paused. 'And Lady Farrar's delighted,' she added deliberately.

'Oh, I understand,' Carly said stormily. 'This is all to do with last New Year's Eve, and the fact that your future father-in-law can't keep his hands to himself. I suspected I hadn't heard the last of that, even though it wasn't my fault, and you know it.'

Sue shrugged again. 'Nevertheless,' she retorted, 'you can hardly expect to be her favourite person.'

'You're quite sure you even want to invite me to the wedding?'

Sue's hesitation was just a fraction too long. 'Don't be silly.'

'I'm not.' Carly rose. 'I think I'm just beginning to see sense.' She gave Sue a long, level look. 'I'm really not wanted here, am I? I'm aware of it more and more each time I come home—that I'm an outsider.'

'Not an outsider,' Sue said angrily. 'A complete stranger—in every way. What do you think it's been like for Mother and Father—for me, listening to people talking about you—about the change in you? Seeing your picture in magazines—on television—all over the place? You know how they've always hated any kind of gossip or notoriety. How they've valued their privacy—their quiet family life. Well, you've ruined that. You've become spectacular, Caro, a media person. But you're not going to spoil my wedding. I want it to be a dignified occasion, not a field-day for a lot of camera-happy idiots.'

'Don't worry about that,' Carly said with supreme bitterness. 'I promise to be somewhere on the other side of the world when that happy dawn breaks. Just let me know what you want as a present, apart from my absence, that is.'

It took all the control she was capable of not to slam the door as she left. She was trembling violently as she walked back to the nursery. She lifted her hands, and began to unfasten her hair, shaking it free on her shoulders in a scented mahogany cloud, scattering the pins piecemeal on the carpet uncaringly.

She knew all about her parents' shock and resentment over her choice of career, and the means she'd chosen to achieve it. That was why she'd tried so hard, each time she returned home, to revert to being plain Caroline Foxcroft in the subordinate role of younger daughter. She thought she'd succeeded on the whole. But clearly she'd made a terrible mistake.

The incident at the New Year party when Sir Giles Farrar, flushed with whisky, had cornered her in the hall, thinking he was unobserved, had been embarrassing, but basically trivial. A more tolerant woman than Lady Farrar would have laughed it off.

Sue would make her the perfect daughter-in-law, she thought, anger stirring within her.

She collected her things, ramming them into her bag with swift, jerky movements. She kept on the grey dress. She could change when she got back to the flat. She didn't want to remain here a minute longer than necessary.

As she carried the case downstairs to the hall, her mother appeared in the drawing-room doorway, Aunt Grace inevitably behind her.

'Caroline?' She stared at the case, raising her brows. 'What are you doing?'

'Leaving,' Carly said briefly. 'Isn't that what everyone wants?'

'Of course not.'

'Well, it's certainly what Susan would prefer.'

'But you can't go,' her mother almost wailed. 'The first guests will be arriving soon. Everyone will think it's so odd.'

Carly shrugged. 'They may also find it relatively eccentric that my own sister doesn't want me as her bridesmaid,' she retorted, her voice brittle.

Mrs Foxcroft sighed. 'So Susan told you. Oh, dear, I rather hoped she'd wait. I knew you'd be upset.'

'That,' Carly said, 'is putting it mildly. Mother, I can't stay for the party, as if nothing had happened. You must see that.'

'Your mother sees nothing of the kind,' said Aunt Grace. 'You're spoiled, Caroline. Spoiled, and selfish. You can hardly wonder that Susan doesn't want you as an attendant. No one's forgotten your behaviour at Louise's wedding.' She snorted. 'Claiming you had a virus only hours before the ceremony—insisting on being taken home, without a thought for anyone but yourself. The balance of the bridal procession was completely destroyed, and it was all your fault. You should have taken an aspirin, and played your part.'

Carly threw back her head. 'Don't tell me I was missed,' she said. 'Louise only asked me because she felt obliged to. It must have been a relief to her not to have me trailing behind her, the ugly duckling among the swans.'

'You were certainly not a prepossessing child,' Aunt Grace said. 'But you've definitely taken drastic steps to remedy the situation since then,' she added disapprovingly. 'I, of course, have never agreed with tampering with nature. And poor Susan must feel it badly, having always been the pretty one.'

'All the more reason for me to go back to London.'

'But everyone will be expecting to see you.' Mrs Foxcroft sounded distracted. 'They'll be asking where you are.'

Carly turned towards the front door. 'Tell them I have another virus,' she flung over her shoulder. 'Or, better still, make it an infectious disease.'

She was still shaking as she drove back along the lanes towards the main road. A tractor pulled out of a gateway ahead of her, and she had to brake sharply to avoid it. She pulled the car over on to the verge, and sat for a few minutes, her arms folded across the steering wheel, and her forehead resting on them, waiting for her heartbeat to steady, trying to regain her equilibrium.

It was stupid to drive when she was so upset, so on edge. She couldn't risk an accident now. It would ruin everything. She had to keep her hard-won beauty intact—flawless.

For Saul Kingsland.

At the thought of him, her whole body tensed uncontrollably.

During those innocent sunlit hours in the garden, prompted by the nostalgic memories of the child she'd been, she'd almost begun to have second thoughts about taking the Flawless assignment. But the confrontation with Susan had hardened her resolve to granite. She still could hardly believe that it had happened, that the girl with whom she'd grown up could resent her so deeply. When they'd been children, they'd been so close, the four-year difference in their ages seeming immaterial.

Sue let me tag around after her everywhere, Carly thought. And I was so proud that she was my big sister. I never minded when people said how lovely she was. I never cared about the comparisons they drew when they looked at us, side by side.

Her throat constricted painfully. But perhaps Susan had enjoyed the contrast, she thought. Even—needed it, to reassure herself about her own looks and popularity. *Mirror, mirror on the wall...* In those days, there'd never been any doubt as to what the mirror would answer.

But then had come Louise's wedding—shattering her—turning everything upside-down. And in its aftermath her whole life had changed—totally and irrevocably.

And with that change had come first bewilderment, then awkwardness and withdrawal, and now, finally, estrangement from her family.

Saul Kingsland, she thought. Saul Kingsland, you have so much to pay for. And I'm going to extract every last penny. Starting now.

The flat seemed emptier than usual as she let herself in. She tossed the case into her room, and went straight to the kitchen. The fridge-freezer held a selection of packet meals which could be microwaved. She chose the first that came to hand, and slid it into the oven.

She filled the coffee percolator, and switched it on. Assembled crockery and cutlery.

Then she went to the telephone. She didn't have to look up the number. She already knew it by heart. She dialled, and waited.

'This is Saul Kingsland.' He sounded, disturbingly, as if he was there in the room with her. 'I'm sorry I can't talk to you in person right now, but if you'd like to leave a message after the tone, I'll get back to you as soon as possible.'

'It's Carly North. If you still want to take some pictures of me, I'm free tomorrow.' She put down the receiver.

That's that, she thought, and went back to the microwave and her instant meal. By the time she'd eaten it, the small kitchen was filled with the aroma of coffee. She poured herself a cup and took it through to the bedroom.

She peeled off the grey dress, and let it fall to the floor. On Monday, she decided, she would take it to a nearly-new shop. Certainly, she never wanted to see it again. She dropped bra, briefs, tights and slip into a linen basket and put on her dressing-gown. Its almost tailored style, with padded shoulders and deep revers, slashed to reveal the cleft between her small, high breasts, was in stark contrast to the sinuous peach satin it was made from. It was the most expensive robe she'd ever bought, but the colour warmed her skin, and acted as a magnificent foil to the tumble of her hair.

Barefoot, she wandered back into the sitting-room and switched on the television set. I don't want anything significant, she told it silently. I just want some mindless entertainment—to prevent me from thinking. Because if I start rehashing every-thing that's happened I shall cry, and I don't want to give way to that kind of weakness.

A film was beginning—a classic thriller which she'd seen many times before—and she subsided into it gratefully, sitting curled up on the sofa, her hands clasped round the warmth of her cup.

It was ridiculous, because it was a beautiful night in early summer, but she still felt chilled to the bone. Perhaps in a minute she would switch on the electric fire.

The sound of the front door buzzer brought her head round sharply. All her circle of friends thought she was at home, enjoying herself at Susan's party.

She got up and trod over to the intercom. 'Yes?' Her voice was not encouraging.

'It's Saul. Open up.'

She had the door half-open before it occurred to her that she had no reason in the world to obey his authoritarian command. But by then it was too late. He was already in the room.

'Isn't it rather late for social calls?' she asked coolly.

'I was intrigued by your message,' he said. 'Also by the fact there were no party sounds in the back-ground. You rang off before I could cut in and talk to you, so I decided to take a chance and come round.' He gave her a narrow-eyed stare. 'What are you doing back so soon from the family reunion?'

Carly shrugged. 'I found I wasn't in a party mood, after all.' She paused. 'If we're going to work together, I hope I'm not going to have to explain every facet of my behaviour.'

'Only if it directly impinges on our relationship.' He was still watching her. 'You look tense.'

'I had a near miss on the drive back,' she said shortly. 'It shook me, rather.' She gave him an edged look. 'Is that sufficient explanation?'

'It will do for now.' He walked forward, dropping the denim jacket he'd been carrying, slung over his shoulder, on to a chair. 'That coffee smells good.'

His jeans were denim too, clinging closely to his lean hips, and long legs, and he wore a plain white shirt, open at the neck, and with the cuffs rolled back to reveal muscular forearms.

'I'm not really in the mood for company.' She stayed by the door, holding it open.

'Then I'll have to change your mood,' he said pleasantly. 'Is the kitchen through there?'

Trembling with temper, she banged the door shut and followed him.

His sudden appearance had unnerved her. She wasn't ready for this kind of intrusion.

She said tautly, 'You really do take over, don't you?'

He poured the coffee into a beaker. 'Tell me what I want to hear, and I'll leave.'

'I—haven't made up my mind yet.'

'Liar,' he said. 'You wouldn't have called me if that were so.'

'I want to wait,' she said, 'until you've photographed me. After all, I might photograph like a dog, and you'd have to change your mind.'

'I've seen how you photograph. This morning I saw some of the work Lonnie Attwood did with you. Now I want you to see yourself through my eyes.'

She shrugged again. 'A rag, a bone and a hank of hair. What's new in that?'

'Some rag.' His eyes slid lazily over her, making her aware without equivocation that he knew she was naked under the robe. 'And some hank, too,' he went on, studying the gleaming waves spilling over her shoulders. 'Is that its natural colour?'

'Hardly.'

'What was it before?'

'Difficult to say. Maybe a sort of—fieldmouse brown.'

'Sounds cute.'

'Very boring, actually.'

He smiled and shook his head. 'Oh, no, lady. Nothing about you could ever be boring. But I approve of Hank Mark Two.'

'I'm sure you do.' Swift, overwhelming anger stung through the words, and he gave her a surprised look.

'Did I say something wrong?'

She wrenched herself back into control. 'Not really. I've had a fraught day, and you're catching the backlash, that's all. When I'm like this, I'm best left in peace.'

'That's one theory.'

'You have a better one?'

He leaned back against the sink unit, very much at ease. His eyes went over her again, slowly, definitively, lingering on the deep V formed by the lapels of her robe, and down to where the satin clung to the line of hip and thigh. She felt her body begin to burn under the long, sensual appraisal. Her breasts seemed swollen and oddly tender as they thrust against their thin covering, and her legs were suddenly like water. Standing there suffering the intimacy of his gaze was a major problem, she thought faintly, so how could she possibly contemplate any other kind of involvement with him, however inconclusive?

'Infinitely better,' he drawled, breaking the thrall of silence she was locked in. 'Making love is a fantastic way of releasing aggression and ironing out the kinks. Pure therapy.'

'Pure,' she said, 'is not the word I'd have chosen.' To her chagrin, her voice sounded very young, and rather breathless.

He grinned at her wickedly. The force of his charm—his attraction, when he chose to exert it, was like being caught in the glare of some arc light, she thought crossly.

'Do I take it you're rejecting my infallible remedy?'

'I'm afraid so.'

'Don't be afraid,' he said. 'That's something you need never be with me. In bed, or out of it.'

'Please don't talk like that.' She felt colour wash into her face.

'Like what?'

'As if it was all a *fait accompli*,' she said wildly. 'As if you were taking over my life.'

'I'll take it by degrees,' he said. 'Starting with your working life. You'll find it completely painless.' He paused. 'I take it your passport's in order?'

'Of course. Why?'

'Because we may be going abroad fairly soon for location work. The Flawless UK chairman, Athol Clement, has suggested that we use his private villa on Thyrsos as a base both for the television commercials and the still shots.'

Her eyes widened. 'Is he serious?'

'Apparently so. He says it's the perfect Greek island—fantastic light, tiny deserted beaches, even a ruined temple. And we'd have the run of it for the duration.' He gave her a meditative look. 'Tempted?'

'It sounds—ideal.'

'Septimus Creed thinks so, too. He wants to get this project off the ground as quickly as possible.'

'You—you said you wouldn't pressure me any more,' she said quickly. 'I'll give you my answer tomorrow. I promise I will.'

'Only now you'd like me to go.'

She nodded mutely.

'Then I suppose I must,' he said ruefully. 'But I'd much rather stay—begin exploring with you exactly what happened between us last night.'

'Nothing happened.' The protest sounded weak.

'Not physically, perhaps. Largely because I didn't trust myself to touch you. But then you already know that, don't you, Carly North?'

She looked down at the floor. 'Yes.'

'A touch of honesty at last,' he said mockingly.

'I'm not usually so evasive.' She tried to smile. 'I think I must still be in shock.' She gave a little helpless shake of the head. 'You see, I'm just not used...' Her voice tailed away.

'That makes two of us.' His expression gentled.

She'd struck the right note, she thought. That hint at her emotional confusion had appealed straight to his masculine ego.

Saul drained the remainder of his coffee, and rinsed the beaker under the tap.

He said abruptly, 'I wish you trusted me.'

'You want so much.'

'In actual fact, I want very little. But I would dearly like to know exactly what went wrong at your country retreat.'

'Oh, that's easily told. A little female squabble over my sister's choice of bridesmaids.'

His brows lifted. 'In other words, you're not one of them.'

'Quite right,' she said with forced lightness. 'I think it must be fate.' She paused, aware that her heart was hammering. 'The last time I was supposed to follow a bride up the aisle,' she went on, keeping her voice casual, 'I was taken ill, hours before the ceremony, and had to drop out. I'd hoped for better luck this time.'

'Only she can't stand the competition,' Saul said, and smiled at her stifled gasp of surprise. 'Well, it's her loss. But it still doesn't explain to my satisfaction the sadness in your eyes.'

'I think you're imagining things,' Carly said defensively. 'I'm tired, that's all.'

He grimaced. 'I suspect that's another hint for me to leave.' He walked across to her, and put a hand under her chin, tilting her face up towards his. He said, 'Goodnight, my elusive beauty. I'll pick you up around ten tomorrow.'

He bent and brushed her mouth with his, swiftly and lightly.

'You see,' he told her softly. 'There's really nothing to fear.'

He went past her, out of the room, and seconds later she heard the front door close behind him.

She lifted a hand and touched her mouth with fingers that shook. Saul's kiss had been so fleeting that it had barely existed, yet she'd felt it in every fibre of her being. Her body was tingling still, and her lips, ridiculously, felt bruised.

Although he'd gone, she realised wonderingly, the room still seemed full of him, as if he'd somehow imprinted his personality on it, indelibly and for all eternity.

Each time I come in here, she thought wildly, I'll see him, lounging there, watching me, his eyes devouring me. When all this is over, I'll have to have the place exorcised—or move.

She walked over to the sink, and picked up the beaker he'd used, studying it curiously as if it was some kind of alien artefact. Delicately, hardly breathing, she ran her finger round the rim where his lips had touched.

Nothing to fear, she thought. Oh, lord, nothing to fear.

And with a little inarticulate cry, she whirled round and threw the beaker at the tiled wall, smashing it beyond repair into a hundred tiny fragments.

CHAPTER FOUR

CARLY was ready an hour before Saul was due to collect her the next morning.

Usually when Lucy was there, Sunday was a lazy day for them both. They got up late, and spent some time lounging with the papers before preparing brunch. But this time she'd been up, it seemed, almost since dawn. She'd tried on half a dozen different outfits, experimented with make-up and her hair, and she still wasn't satisfied.

In the end, she put on a simple white cotton dress, sleeveless, and flaring gently from a deep yoke, and tied her hair back with a matching ribbon. She used eye-shadow and blusher with discretion, accentuating eyes and cheekbones with an artist's hand.

He'd seen her sophisticated, and next door to naked. Today it would be the virginal look, she thought detachedly, surveying her handiwork.

When she opened the door to him, his brows lifted slightly, but he made no comment.

'So, where are we going—Hyde Park?' she asked, as she sat beside him in the car, the sun pouring through the windows.

'A rather more peaceful environment than that.' He slanted her a swift smile. 'I hope you have no plans for the rest of the day.'

'Nothing definite.' She kept her tone neutral, in spite of an inner stab of alarm.

'Good,' Saul said laconically, and slid the car expertly through a gap in the traffic.

She was on tenterhooks to see the route he would take, but when she realised it was nowhere near the road she had followed yesterday she began imperceptibly to relax, although she still had no idea where they were going.

They didn't talk much, but Carly was aware of Saul's brief sidelong glance flicking towards her constantly as he drove.

And I should be watching him too, she thought. Persuading him with every half-smile, every flutter of my eyelashes, that my interest in him is real, and personal. Oh, I wish I was a better actress.

She was thankful when there was no city left, and she could concentrate with genuine interest on the scenery. She thought for a while that they were going to the coast, but Saul soon left the main road, and turned the car into a maze of lanes.

Drawing her deeper and deeper into some web of his own devising, she thought, but who was the one who would remain caught when it was all over?

She drew a deep breath, and felt him look at her again more sharply. To cover it, she said lightly, 'Will we ever find our way back?'

'Would it matter?'

She shrugged. 'I think we might be missed. Clive would be looking for his percentage.' She paused. 'And I'm sure someone, somewhere is keeping tabs on you.'

'A thankless task.' He was smiling.

'I'm sure it is.' She moved her shoulders, luxuriating in the sun's warmth. 'What a heavenly day.'

'And you're going to enjoy it in a tiny corner of Paradise.'

'No other clues?'

'I thought you'd like a touch of mystery.' The hedgerows they were driving between were bright with hawthorn. Carly could have extended a hand and picked some as they passed. 'After all,' he went on, 'you're something of an enigma yourself.'

Her heart missed a beat. 'Nonsense.' She extended slender bare arms. 'Nothing up my sleeves—look.'

'I'm looking all the time,' he said. 'I'm just not sure what I see.'

She forced a laugh. 'Well, they say the camera cannot lie.'

'It's not obliged to tell the whole truth, either.' His tone was wry. 'All in all, it promises to be an interesting day.' He paused. 'Are you hungry?'

'Yes, I am,' she admitted, slightly surprised. She'd made herself some toast back in that early daylight, but thrown most of it away.

'Then we'll eat.'

There was a signpost indicating a village half a mile ahead. It was a tiny place, just a few houses and a church clustering round the edge of a green, and the inevitable pub. There was already a handful of cars parked outside, and people were standing, or sitting in the sun, drinks in hand.

'It could be just bread and cheese,' Saul warned, as he swung himself out of the car.

'That would be wonderful,' she said. 'With a lager.'

She found the last vacant table, and sat down. He'd said, 'the rest of the day', she thought. What did that mean? How long did a day last, and what did he have planned for its ending? After all, they'd admitted a mutual attraction. She could hardly express outrage if he expected her to remain with him through the night.

She bit her lip. I'm going to have to be so careful, she thought.

'Still brooding over your family problems?' Saul put down the lagers, and sat beside her on the wooden bench, his thigh brushing hers.

'I'm sorry, does it show?' She resisted the impulse to edge away.

'I'm glad that it does. You don't need to hide things from me.' He was smiling as he said it, but Carly found her body tingling under the sudden intensity of his regard.

She ran her finger down the condensation on the outside of her glass. 'Am I allowed no secrets at all?'

Saul shook his head slowly. 'No,' he said quietly. 'I want to know everything.'

'That sounds—alarming.'

'It doesn't have to be instant knowledge. Learning should be a gradual and enjoyable process.' The caress in his voice was almost tangible, as if his hands had touched her intimately. 'I hope that you want to know about me, too. That I'm not just someone who can further your career.'

'No,' she said. 'No, I don't see you like that at all.'

'Good.' He took her free hand and carried it to his lips. 'Although I plan to make you the sensation of the year—of the decade.'

She pouted laughingly, covering up the swift, unwanted flare of sensation which the brush of his mouth across her skin had induced. 'Not the century?'

'That too,' he promised solemnly. 'Now, here comes our bread and cheese.'

It was more than that, of course. A waitress brought twin platters loaded with cheese, and slices of home-cured ham, flanked by chunks of french bread and a crisp salad, and accompanied by an assortment of chutneys and pickles. In spite of her inner turmoil, Carly found she was eating ravenously.

When they'd finished their meal, Saul walked her round the green to the church. There was an ancient lych gate, and beyond it in the churchyard a yew tree, its trunk thickened with the centuries, its boughs almost sweeping the ground.

Saul made her stand in front of it while he photographed her, a slim, pale shape against the tree's darkness, the faint breeze lifting her hair, and ruffling the white dress into a cloud.

He directed her sharply and succinctly, ordering every turn of her body, every motion of her head, making her kick off her sandals and stand barefoot and on tiptoe, as if about to take flight.

'Fantastic,' he said, finally, telling her to rest. 'Like Primavera—or Persephone escaping from the gates of Hell.'

'That was relatively painless,' she commented, slipping on her sandals again. 'I'd heard you were a terrible bully.'

'I can be,' he said. 'And the session's only just begun. We're off to a new location, that's all.'

His stride was long, and she had to trot to catch up with him. 'Are you leaving the car?'

'It's within walking distance.' He took her down a narrow lane, where the trees met overhead to form a sun-dappled canopy. The cottage was at the bottom of a short slope, set back from the road. It was an attractive building, whitewashed and half-timbered, with moss gathering on the roof tiles. Rambler roses and wistaria reached up to the first-floor windows in an ordered tangle.

'Like it?' Saul smiled at her bemused expression.

She drew a breath. 'It's fabulous. How did you know it was here?'

'I know the owner.' He pushed open the gate.

Carly hung back, giving him a suspicious look. 'Is it yours, by any chance?'

He laughed. 'No, I've never put down roots like this. But it's all right, she's away, and anyway, she wouldn't mind.'

Wouldn't she? Carly thought as she followed him round the side of the house, and through another wicket gate. Then she must be very tolerant. I wonder precisely who 'she' is?

Then, when she saw what was confronting her, she stopped wondering about anything, and just stood, filling her eyes with its beauty.

Beyond the confines of the cottage garden was the bank of a stream, and there someone had planted masses of azaleas, which were now blooming in full maturity, a carpet of vibrant scarlets, pinks and mauves all the way to the water's edge. The colours were almost a shock to the senses, she thought faintly.

'Stunned?' He came to stand beside her. 'I always am, too. I keep telling myself it can't possibly be as I remember, and yet it always is.' He put his arm round her, drawing her against him. 'As soon as I saw you, I wanted to put you in this setting.'

She gave a nervous laugh. 'It's too lovely. I don't deserve it.'

'You'll enhance it.' He turned her fully into his arms, looking down into her face. He gave a small, uneven laugh. 'Oh, Carly,' he said softly, 'I brought you here to work...'

He bent his head, and his mouth came down on hers. This time, his kiss was neither casual nor gentle. His lips were hungry, parting hers in an aching demand which would not be denied. His tongue invading her mouth, seeking her sweetness, was like silk—but silk that burned, she thought dazedly as the sunlight, the azaleas, the dazzle on the water and Saul's kiss became some sweet and fiery unity that threatened to consume her.

His hands stroked her back, tracing the supple length of her spine through the thin fabric of her dress, and her body arched towards his in startled and imploring delight.

He said huskily, 'Oh, my sweet,' and pulled her against him, moulding her body to his, making her aware that he was fiercely and heatedly aroused. At the same time, his hand sought the zip at the back of her dress.

The force of that realisation jerked her back to some semblance of reality. Her hands lifted in panic, pushing at his chest, thrusting him away from her.

'No,' she choked from her dry throat. 'Let go of me.'

He obeyed instantly. She took a step backwards, lips parting to drag air into her lungs, arms folding defensively across her body.

Faint colour burned along his cheekbones, and his mouth twisted as he noted the gesture. He said, 'Carly, you don't have to worry. In spite of appearances, I haven't brought you here to rape you.' He shrugged almost wryly. 'I hadn't planned on seduction either, but you were so—exquisitely responsive. I—lost my head for a moment.'

And she had lost hers too, she thought, in horrified disbelief. For a moment, she had forgotten everything, almost drowning in a pleasure that was totally new to her experience. Oh, how could it have happened—how could she have allowed it to happen—and with Saul Kingsland, of all the men on earth?

'I'm so ashamed.'

She didn't realise she'd spoken aloud until she saw his brows snap together.

'There's nothing to feel shame about. The point of no return was still a long way off. Surely you realise that.' He paused with a sharp intake of breath. 'Or don't you know? Is that what you're trying to tell me? That you haven't—that there's never...?'

She lifted her chin. 'Is it so impossible to believe?'

'No,' he said quietly. 'Suddenly it's not impossible at all. In fact, it explains a great deal.' He threw back his head and looked at her, almost dispassionately. 'But what I can't figure,' he went on, 'is why? You're beautiful, and you certainly aren't frigid, so why hasn't there been someone for you?'

She turned away, looking across the rioting azaleas to the gleam of the water. 'There were always other priorities,' she said slowly. 'My career, for instance.'

And my revenge.

'But that isn't all.' His hands descended on her shoulders, holding her lightly and without threat. He said gently, 'I think at some time, Carly North, you've been hurt quite badly. I think it's made you wary—made you close in on yourself. Made you shut out other people. Well, I'm telling you that's all over now.'

'You're going to heal me?' Her face felt as if it had been turned to stone. She was glad that he was standing behind her, and couldn't see her expression.

'I'm going to try.' He paused. 'It would help if you could tell me a little about it . . .'

'Not now,' she said. 'But one day I'll tell you. I promise I will.'

'Then I'll be satisfied with that.' His lips touched her hair. 'So don't go tense on me again. From now on, we play this your way. I won't force the pace, or make any demands you're not ready for.'

'You're—very understanding, and very kind.'

'A misunderstood saint, in fact.' Amusement quivered in his voice. 'Don't be fooled, lady, I'm not that altruistic. I'm hoping that if I'm patient with you now, one of these days all that dammed-up passion is going to break through, and you're going to give yourself to me without holding back. In fact, I'm counting on it.' He turned her to face him. 'And, as you don't yet want my body, I'm going to make love to you with my camera instead. Go and sit among the flowers.'

She obeyed, smiling, lifting her face to the sun. Without knowing it, Saul had just delivered into her hands the perfect weapon to use against him.

His patience, she thought, his self-control, tried to the utmost limits. Oh, how she could make him suffer.

And I will, she promised silently, picking a handful of crimson blossoms and tossing them in the air so that the petals drifted down over her face and dress. I will.

He said, 'Tell me now, lady. Are you going to take the assignment—become my Flawless Girl?'

She looked at him, her face wiped of all emotion except that radiant professional smile. And said once again, but aloud this time, 'I will.'

She sat beside him in the car, as they drove back into London, feeling totally drained. It had been a long, demanding session, and Saul had been unsparing with her, driving her relentlessly to give more of herself than she had with any other photographer.

When she'd tried to protest at one point, he'd said shortly, 'I'm not interested in pretty masks, darling. I want the woman beneath, or nothing at all.'

But, exhausted as she was, she had to admit, reluctantly, that she had never felt more stimulated or more alive during a session.

Working with Saul Kingsland could have been the experience of a lifetime, she thought, with a tinge of regret, instantly subdued.

He said, 'Will you have dinner with me tonight?'

'I—can't. I have a prior invitation—from Clive and Marge.'

It wasn't true, but Clive and Marge always kept open house on Sunday evenings, and people were welcome to drop in if they chose. There was nearly always a crowd, talking endlessly, playing music and silly card games, helping themselves from the huge pots of spaghetti and chili con carne in the kitchen.

Carly always enjoyed herself there, but tonight their home would be a refuge. Because she'd been shocked to realise how tempted she'd been to accept Saul's invitation, and let her day with him linger into evening, and beyond. The clean, warm taste of his mouth exploring hers, the stroke of his hands, the stark pressure of his lean body—all these returned to haunt her with total recall.

Because—just for a moment—she had been in genuine danger, much as she loathed to admit it, her untried flesh awakened and urgent.

And now she was tired, and therefore vulnerable. Apart from anything else, she'd allowed herself to enjoy their working rapport too much, she castigated herself. So it would be altogether unwise to risk spending any more time in his company.

He might be her enemy, but he was wickedly, frighteningly attractive, she thought broodingly, and she was going to need all her strength and all her wits about her to resist him physically and emotionally.

'Are you going to tell Clive your decision? Naturally Septimus Creed will contact him with the contract details.' Saul paused. 'You know the snags, I suppose. Exclusive rights to you. No pictures of you, other than as the Flawless Girl, to appear anywhere for the duration of the agreement.'

'Yes,' she said. 'I know.'

'I hope you do,' he said, a shade grimly. 'The company has invested a lot of money in pre-publicity—the search to find The Girl, and are spending even more on the campaign. If there was any kind of foul-up, they could get nasty.'

'Then I'll have to be ultra-careful.'

'We both will.' He drew up the car outside her block, and looked at her, reaching to draw his forefinger lightly round the curve of her lower lip. 'Sure I can't persuade you to change your mind, and stay with me this evening?' he asked quietly. 'It's dinner that's on offer. Nothing more.'

'I—know that, but it's still impossible.' She looked down at her hands, folded tightly in her lap. 'I'm sorry.'

'So am I.' His voice was rueful. 'But I can wait.'

When she got into the flat, her heart was hammering as if she'd taken part in some marathon, and she sagged weakly against the closed panels of the door, fighting to control her breathing.

Other men—men she'd liked—had kissed her, and she'd found it pleasant, without experiencing the kind of stir in her blood which would have tempted her to go beyond kissing.

So why must it be Saul Kingsland, whom she hated, who could make the lightest caress matter so terribly? It had taken all her will-power, she recognised, dry-mouthed, to walk away from him into the building.

Perhaps it was some kind of karma, she thought. A divine retribution being exacted in advance for what she was going to do to him.

She said aloud, 'Well, so be it.'

Marge said, 'You look different.'

Carly concentrated her attention on the bottle of wine she was opening. 'Different better, I hope.'

'I'm not sure.'

Carly sent her a glance of mock horror. 'Marge, darling, I'm going to be the Flawless Girl. Now is not the moment to tell me that my looks are going off.'

'I wasn't going to,' Marge said drily. 'You're as stunning as ever. All the single men here tonight are drooling with lust—and a few of the married ones too.' She paused. 'No, it's something in your eyes—a faraway look you get—as if you had some secret you were hugging to yourself.' She added deliberately, 'And I'd be much happier, Carly my sweet, if I thought it was a nice secret.'

Carly managed a careless laugh. 'You have a great imagination, Marge. No wonder you were such a whiz as a copywriter.'

'I wish it was just imagination,' Marge said with a measuring look. 'Are you planning to pour that wine, or just strangle the bottle with your bare hands?' She paused again. 'Did I see you chatting to Mark Clayfield earlier?'

'Do I hear your disapproval showing?'

'Yes, you do, actually.' Marge filled a bowl with crisps.

'Then why do you have him here, if he's *persona non grata*?'

Marge sighed. 'Because he and Clive were at university together, and he used to be a half-way decent journalist before he sold himself to that terrible Sunday rag. Now I feel I have to guard every word in front of him, in case they appear in the next edition as "bored housewife's kinky fantasies".'

'Well, I didn't say a word he could use against me,' Carly said. 'In fact, I found him quite pleasant.'

Marge snorted. 'No doubt he wants you to strip for that centrefold of his. Become one of his Sunday Sirens.'

Carly bent her head, letting her hair swing forward like a curtain. 'My goodness, can you imagine Clive's face?'

'Indeed I can, and not only his.' Marge tipped peanuts into a variety of small dishes, and put them on a tray. 'Following on from that, how did you enjoy dinner with Saul Kingsland?'

'It was fine.' Carly bit her lip. 'Do you think I should open another bottle of white wine?'

'On past experience, I'd open several. Is "fine" all you have to say on the subject?'

Carly shrugged neutrally. 'I've achieved my ambition,' she returned. 'He's taken my photograph. And he's going to take more.'

'Ah, yes,' said Marge. 'I suppose congratulations are in order. If the Flawless assignment is really what you want, of course.'

Carly opened her eyes wide. 'How could it not be? It's going to make me the most famous face in Europe.'

'For a little while, certainly,' Marge conceded ironically. 'What are you going to do as an encore?'

'I'll worry about that when the time comes.' Carly picked up the tray of glasses. 'I'd better take these round before they all go purple and their tongues start to swell.'

For goodness' sake, she thought, as she carried the tray into the big, comfortable cluttered drawing-room. It's as if she knows. But she can't. No one has the least inkling. She's just fishing.

But that was unfair. Marge had been a friend to her from those first, uncertain days when she'd tested whether her face was going to be her fortune or not. She'd been more of an older sister, more of a mother to Carly than the real incumbents of those positions. And her antennae were second to none. She knew there was something wrong— something off-key—and she was concerned.

And when it was over she would be devastated.

I wish I could tell her, Carly thought, as she laughed and chatted and passed round wine. I wish I could confide in her. But I daren't. Because she'd tell Clive, and that would be the end of it. And I've waited too long to allow that to happen.

In fact, it seems to have used up all my life— waiting for Saul to come back.

CHAPTER FIVE

As she was passing through the hall on her way back to the kitchen, Clive was coming down the stairs.

'I bear ill tidings,' he said. 'The Third Monster is asking for you. Claims the last time you were here, you promised to read her a story. Absolutely refuses to go to sleep without it.'

'Yes, I did,' Carly said remorsefully. 'I'll go right up.'

In the room at the far end of the landing, Laura was sitting up in bed, clutching a favourite teddy bear, her eyes turned expectantly towards the door.

'You've been such a long time,' she complained, lifting her face for Carly's kiss. 'Teddy's gone to sleep already.'

'Then I'll have to read specially quietly so as not to wake him.' Carly looked at the pile of books on the night table. 'What story is it to be?'

'*The Ugly Duckling,*' Laura said promptly. 'And will you act all the bits like you always do?'

'Yes,' Carly said gently. 'I'll act all the bits.'

The familiar tale of rejection and ultimate joy wound its familiar course, and Laura listened avidly, her eyelids drooping as Carly, her voice softening, reached the conclusion.

'I'm glad the other swans liked him,' she said sleepily, leaning her head against Carly's arm.

'What would he have done, poor thing, if they hadn't wanted him either?'

'I don't know sweetheart,' Carly said huskily. 'I really don't know.'

'Perhaps he'd have become something else instead,' Laura said. 'Something he didn't want to be...' Her voice trailed away, and her eyes closed.

Carly felt the sudden sting of tears against her own eyelids. Perhaps so, she thought. Perhaps so, indeed.

She knew from past experience that Laura, once asleep, would not stir, and there was nothing to prevent her from putting the little girl back on her pillows and rejoining the party downstairs.

Yet she felt in no hurry to do so. She stayed where she was, enjoying the peace in the room, the soft sounds of the child's breathing. Up to now, she'd seen and appreciated what Clive and Marge had in their marriage without envy. But, suddenly, she found herself wondering what it would be like to have a child of her own. To conceive it, protect it inside her body, and give it birth and love it.

She'd never even considered such an eventuality before, she thought wonderingly. She'd been too determined, too single-minded in her purpose to allow the possibility of a different kind of future for herself. So why was she thinking about it now, just when the victory she'd dreamed of was almost within her grasp? Surely she couldn't be weakening, now of all times?

She heard a small sound and, turning her head, saw Saul standing in the doorway staring at her. For a moment, she thought he was a figment of her imagination—a mirage created out of the mass of confused emotion within her, then he took a step forward into the room, and she knew he was only too real, and gasped, her hand flying to her throat.

Disturbed by the sudden movement, Laura muttered something, turning her head restlessly. Carly hesitated, then eased herself away from the child, lowering her on to the pillows and tucking the covers round her.

Saul was waiting for her on the landing. 'I seem to spend my life startling you,' he said wryly.

'What are you doing here?' She was angry, and more shaken by his sudden appearance than she wanted to be. 'How dare you do this? Are you following me—checking up on me for some reason?'

'Of course not, what do you take me for?' His brows drew together. 'Clive telephoned me to say you'd told him the news, and that although he still didn't approve he was putting some champagne on ice. He invited me over to share the celebration. Didn't he mention it?'

'No, he didn't.' Carly bit her lip hard.

'Then maybe he should have done,' Saul said coolly, 'as there's clearly some problem. But I can always leave, if that's what you'd prefer.'

He turned towards the stairs, and she flew after him. 'No—Saul, please.' She tugged at the sleeve of his jacket. 'I'm sorry I came on so strong, but I just wasn't expecting to see you there. Of course we must celebrate. It was a marvellous idea of Clive's.'

'Was it?' There was no softening in his dark face. 'I'll have to take your word for that, lady.'

She threw back her head. 'I've said I'm sorry. What do you want me to do—grovel?'

'No,' he said. 'Explain.' He shrugged. 'But I'm aware that's not possible, so we'll leave it there. Now I'll go down, drink Clive's champagne and go.'

She said in a low voice. 'That's—not what I want.'

Saul gave her a long look. When he spoke, his voice was slightly more gentle. 'Are you sure you really know?'

She nodded mutely. She couldn't let him walk away like this. Couldn't risk the possibility of a rift which might ruin everything. Not now.

For a moment he was still, then he shrugged again, and extended his hand. She put hers into it, and they walked downstairs together.

Clive's speech hailing Carly as the Flawless Girl was a masterpiece. The majority of his audience were left with the belief that it was all his own idea, and that it was due to his ceaseless efforts that she was fronting the campaign at all. Saul's gaze was ironic as it met hers.

They were, naturally, the centre of attention. But, as they laughed and talked, Carly was aware of a continuing reserve in Saul's manner towards her. She was conscious too of the buzz of excitement his arrival had created among the women present, and soon found, not altogether to her surprise, that he'd been cornered by one of Marge's actress neighbours. Mel Bolton was blonde, ambitious and predatory, and while her use of body language might not be subtle it was certainly effective, Carly thought grimly, observing from the corner of her eye how Mel's slender finger was playing idly with the buttons on Saul's shirt, while she smiled beguilingly up at him.

Saul's response was rather more difficult to fathom. Glass in hand, lounging back against the wall, he looked relaxed, and faintly amused. But Carly could swear there was growing appreciation in his eyes as they studied the cling of Mel's seductive little black dress.

'At the moment, he's just flattered,' Marge said in her ear. 'But I've seen Mel in action too often. Give her another twenty minutes, and he'll be leaving with her.'

Oh, no, he won't, Carly said silently, feeling her nails curling like claws into the palms of her hands.

That was something she hadn't allowed for—the intervention of another woman to muddy the waters and provide another focus for Saul's attention. And it was something she needed to deal with.

She walked over, and slid her hand through his arm, giving Mel Bolton a swift smile.

'Saul, can I possibly drag you away? All that fresh air this afternoon seems to have knocked me out, and I'd like to go home now.'

Saul said equably, 'Very well,' but the quizzical lift of his brows was a challenge.

As they crossed the room, he said softly, 'Leading me out of temptation, darling? I wasn't aware you required my services as an escort tonight.'

She flushed slightly. 'I—I need to talk to you. To find out more about the assignment. This trip to Thyrsos, for instance—is it definitely on?'

'A matter of supreme importance indeed,' he commented sardonically. 'And the answer is, yes, as far as I know. We'll probably get final confirmation in a day or two.'

As she sat beside him in the car, she said jerkily, 'You still haven't forgiven me, have you?'

'For what? For preventing my acceptance of the rather obvious invitation I was getting?' The glance he sent her was edged.

'Of course not,' she said too quickly. 'You're a free agent, after all. No, I meant for—sounding off at you as I did.'

'Well, let's leave it at that,' he said, after a pause. 'You're tired, and my sudden appearance was a shock to you. End of story.'

'I'm not usually this temperamental. Anyone will tell you that.'

'They have. You have a name for being totally professional and co-operative.'

He was still, she realised, keeping her at a distance. And that was bad news. She needed him involved—under any spell she cared to weave.

When they arrived outside the flat, she said, 'Would you like to come in for a drink—some coffee, perhaps?'

'I think I should let you get an early night instead.'

'It doesn't have to be—that immediate.'

He was silent for a moment, then he said, 'In that case, fine. I could use some coffee.'

This time, he stayed in the sitting-room while she made it and carried it through. She found him down on one knee, scrutinising her record collection.

'They say you can tell a person's character by studying the books they have on their shelves,' he said over his shoulder. 'I wonder if it's the same with music?'

'What does it tell you?' She sat down on the sofa.

'On the surface, fairly conventional.' He came to sit beside her. 'But underneath, a romantic streak which upbringing and conditioning hasn't been able to subdue, and a tendency to take risks. Hidden depths, and some surprising contradictions.' He paused. 'How am I doing, so far?'

She shrugged. 'You make me sound far more interesting than I really am.'

'Not just interesting,' he said. 'Fascinating.'

She poured the coffee and handed it to him.

'It's a very pleasant flat. How did you acquire it?' he asked.

'I was very fortunate. I had a wealthy godmother. When she died, I found she'd left me quite a lot of money. I inherited it when I was eighteen.'

'And invested in this place?'

'Among other things.'

'A wise move. Property prices round here look set to go through the ceiling.'

'That doesn't really concern me. I'm not planning on selling.'

'So, what are your plans?'

She gave a slight shrug. 'I—seem to fall in with whatever life throws at me.'

'And right now, it's hurled the Flawless contract into your lap. Your face on hoardings, in magazine spreads and television commercials. Personal appearances at stores and beauty centres up and down the country, and across the Channel.'

'You make it sound—rather daunting.'

'But also extremely lucrative. Most of the models I've met are looking to the future, squirrelling away their earnings into some kind of business which will keep them when their faces are no longer their fortunes. Have you thought about that?'

No, she thought. Because everything I've done, every decision I've made, has had only one aim in mind—to bring you down—and I've never looked beyond that.

She shrugged again. 'Oh, I think I have a few good years left.'

'I'd say you had any number of spectacular years,' Saul said drily, putting down his empty cup. 'Thank you for the coffee. I shall now leave you in peace.'

She didn't look at him. Slowly she replaced her own cup on the table, beside his. 'Do you—really have to go so soon?'

She could sense the sudden tension in his lean body. 'No.'

She leaned back against the cushions. 'Well, then...'

As he bent towards her, she closed her eyes, sliding her arms up round his neck, drawing him down against her pliant body.

For a while, she remained passive while his mouth gently caressed hers, then, aware that he was about to lift his head, she delicately flicked her tongue along his lower lip.

Immediately Saul's arms tightened around her, and with a faint groan he deepened the kiss to passionate demand. She responded instantly, exploring his mouth with the same urgent intensity, stroking the hair at the nape of his neck with fingers that shook.

His weight was pressing her down into the softness of the sofa. Every bone, every muscle, every nerve-ending was aware of him. She felt the pulsing of his heart against her own.

His hand lifted, touched her breast through the jade and turquoise silk of her shirt. She felt her nipples peaking eagerly under the brush of his fingers and gasped.

Beware, a voice in her brain screamed at her. It's his self-control you're testing, not your own. This should stop here and now.

He lifted himself away and looked down at her, his eyes guarded, watchful, the lean body tense as whipcord. Her skin was tingling, greedy for his touch, as slowly—too slowly—Saul began to release the buttons on her shirt from their fastenings. His hands lingered on their task—even fumbled a little, as if he was uncertain or afraid.

She didn't want this gentle, almost tentative wooing, she thought dazedly. She wanted him excited, hungry for her, demanding—something she could turn against him into reproach when the time came to call a halt.

A heavy silence enfolded them. She could hear neither her own breathing nor his. Her consciousness, her entire being, seemed concentrated on the unhurried movement of his hands. The rustle of the silk sounded almost harsh in her ears as he pushed the shirt from her shoulders at last.

As his hands cupped her nakedness, her heated flesh seemed to surge beneath his fingers. Her whole body clenched suddenly in one agonising pulse of desire.

'Oh, Carly.' There was pain in his brief words, and yearning too, and when he kissed her again his mouth took hers with stark sensuality.

His hands stroked her breasts, fondling the rosy peaks lightly but sensuously, sending small ripples of a new and painful delight through her body. Making her achingly aware that Saul's caresses were engendering other desires, other needs, unfamiliar, but disturbingly potent.

She found herself wondering crazily what it would be like to have him touch her everywhere—to have his mouth and hands making a feast of her. The thought sent a shaft of longing piercing through her, so intense it made her moan out loud. Her arms locked fiercely round his neck, and her slender hips lifted, sharply, involuntarily to strain against his own.

'That's enough.' The words seemed to come from a million miles away, as if they'd been torn out of him.

Saul jackknifed away from her, flinging himself to the end of the sofa furthest from her. For a moment he sat motionless, eyes closed, trying to steady his breathing.

Then he said again, 'That's enough.'

'Why?' Carly hardly recognised her own voice. Could not believe she was asking the question.

'Because we either stop now, or we finish it in bed.' He saw her flinch from the sudden harshness in his voice, and added more gently, 'And I don't think you're ready for that. Not yet.' He paused. 'Are you?'

Slowly, mutely, she shook her head.

'That's what I thought.' He sounded resigned, almost grim, but he sent her the beginnings of a smile. 'For heaven's sake, lady, have you the slightest idea what you do to me?' He raked a hand through his hair, then leaned forward, pulling her shirt back into place, his mouth twisting ruefully as he tugged the edges across her bare breasts.

His hand touched her face, stroking the curve of her cheek. He said quietly, 'I can't kiss you again. I don't trust myself. So I'll just say goodnight and go.'

At the door, he turned and looked back at her. He spoke softly, a note in his voice of laughter and promise.

'A word of warning, my lovely one. When it finally happens, one or both of us may not survive.'

The door closed behind him, and she was alone.

For a while, she couldn't move, couldn't think, then slowly and stiffly she sat up, forcing the buttons of her shirt back into their holes with shaking fingers, trying to come to terms with the near-disaster which had befallen her.

For a brief while, in Saul's arms, she'd forgotten everything that had motivated her—driven her inexorably for the past five years. Put out of her mind the mental suffering he'd caused her, and the long months of physical pain which had resulted, which she'd deliberately invited.

He'd almost destroyed her. Now she intended to destroy him. It was that simple. So, how could she have allowed it to slip away from her consciousness even for a minute?

And all for a few moments of sexual pleasure—
the most transient experience known to the human
race, she thought in self-derision.

But what had she expected? When she set out to
play with fire, she could hardly complain when she
was the one who was scorched.

She'd thought that everything she'd once felt for
Saul was dead—eclipsed, stifled at birth by his un-
thinking cruelty. And that, at best, it had been a
naïve, adolescent stirring of emotion. Now, she realised, it was not so easily dismissed. When she'd
first met Saul Kingsland—first fallen so headily and
dizzily in love with him—she'd been a child on the
threshold of womanhood, with a woman's needs,
a woman's desires. And, while love had turned to
disillusion and hatred, she had to face the un-
welcome fact that desire could continue and co-exist
along with that hatred.

A long shudder ran through her as she leaned
back against the cushions, wrapping her arms round
her body, feeling the sour ache of unsatisfied
arousal deep within her.

She needed to blot that out. Needed to block the
memory of Saul's hands and lips on her skin with
other more powerful remembrances.

I don't want to remember, she thought, wincing.
But I must.

She had to probe once more at those five-year-
old scars. Provide herself with a final, dark reminder of what she had become, and why.

Let her mind take her back, yet again, to the
tranquil summer day when it had all begun.

* * *

'Isn't it fantastic?' said Louise, her hair a golden aureole in the sun which poured through the window. 'Saul Kingsland, of all people, agreeing to photograph the wedding.' She gave a little laugh. 'When James told me, I could hardly believe it.'

Five of her bridesmaids, gathered in her bedroom for the final fitting of their dresses, looked and murmured their envy. Caroline, the sixth, and youngest, knowing that she was not required to give an opinion, stood patiently while Mrs Barlow and her assistant twitched irritably at the folds of fabric which enveloped her, and exchanged tight-lipped glances.

'How on earth did James get to know him?' Sue sprawled on the bed and helped herself from a box of chocolates. 'Saul must be years older than he is.'

'Only about five. They were at school together. Saul was James's head of house, and captain of the first eleven, and heaven knows what else. James absolutely hero-worshipped him when he was young. And then, when Alex was killed in that ambush in Northern Ireland, Saul was incredibly kind and supportive. Kept James from cracking up, and made him see that joining the army in his brother's place, and maybe getting himself killed in turn, was no answer.' She gave a slight, guilty giggle. 'For which he has my undying gratitude. And, of course, he and James have kept in touch since.'

'You are lucky, Louise,' Katie Arnold said with a sigh.

'Well, there are strings, of course. He doesn't want to take just the stock shots. He's thinking of bringing out a book—a complete record of a country wedding, warts and all.' Louise giggled again. 'Mummy wasn't awfully pleased when I told her he'd be arriving later today to snap her bawling out the caterers yet again over the phone.'

'Is he going to photograph us trying on our dresses?' Belinda Knox asked eagerly. 'I wish I'd worn my Janet Reger camiknickers.'

'You'll be lucky if any of you get to try your dresses with the time Caroline is taking,' Louise said with a shrug. 'What's the problem, Mrs Barlow?'

'It's the length, Miss Brotherton. We seem to have gained another inch and a half.'

'Caro's having one of her droopy days,' Sue said lightly. 'Do stand up straight, darling, and try and co-operate. You're keeping everyone waiting.'

Caroline sighed inwardly, and straightened herself, aware that a painful blush was spreading up from her toes.

It was all right for Sue. She and the others were the same relative height.

But I'm half a head taller, she thought forlornly. Everyone will notice when we all walk up the aisle. Her glasses were slipping, and she pushed them back up her nose with the little nervous gesture which had become a habit.

Mrs Barlow tutted. 'If you could manage to stand still, also, Miss Foxcroft.'

'Yes, for heavens's sake, Caro,' Louise said crossly, 'we do all have other things to do, you know. Mrs Barlow, I'm still not sure about the neck detail on my gown. It looked wonderful on the Princess of Wales, I agree, but...'

Mrs Barlow immediately sprang to the defence of her design, and Caroline was thankful to have attention diverted away from her own shortcomings.

She'd been so excited when Louise had invited her to be a bridesmaid, but it hadn't been a totally happy experience so far. As the youngest, she felt very much an outsider. Very much still the schoolgirl, while her cousin, her sister and their friends seemed like women of the world.

They even looked alike, she thought, as if they'd been picked from a matching set. Whereas she . . .

She stole a sideways glance at herself in the long mirror, and frowned. She didn't want to stand straight. When she bent her head a little, she could convince herself that her long nose was slightly less obtrusive. And if she hunched her shoulders no one could tell that her breasts hadn't really budded under the draped mauve chiffon bodice, but had to be helped with a padded bra. If only she could put on some weight.

She stifled another sigh. 'Could I have a chocolate, Sue?'

'Certainly not. You know what sweets do to you. The last thing you want is one of your horrible spots in time for the ceremony. Do have a bit of sense.'

The tone of her sister's voice made Caroline realise it would be wiser to stand tall, allow Mrs Barlow to make whatever adjustments were needed, and then take herself off somewhere, out of everyone's way.

But it was a good half-hour later before she could have her wish, and, dressed once more in the comfortable anonymity of jeans and T-shirt, run downstairs, and out into the sunlight. Reuben, Aunt Grace's golden retriever, followed her. He seemed to feel out of place in all the hectic preparations too, she thought, stroking his head.

'Come on, old boy,' she whispered. 'We'll go for a walk down by the river.'

It was a blissful time, that last golden hour of her childhood, at the water's edge. She found a stick and threw it for the dog, and let him bring it back to her over and over again, until they were both soaked and muddy.

Reuben had the stick in his jaws, and was half crouching, growling in mock menace, his damp, plumy tail waving in delight, while Caroline, laughing, tried to wrest it from him, when she heard a sound that was an intrusion, wholly unconnected with their game, or the lapping of the water, and the breeze in the trees. A buzz, followed by a click.

She looked round, and saw him, a young man, a stranger, a few yards away, camera poised.

'Don't stop,' he ordered peremptorily. 'Pretend I'm not here.'

She couldn't. She was frozen with embarrassment and, when she did move, it was to make that swift, self-conscious adjustment to her glasses.

'Damnation,' he said ruefully, and put his camera away. 'I hoped I'd manage a few more shots before you saw me. You were having such a marvellous time, and I've spoiled it.'

'It—doesn't matter.' She got quickly to her feet, wiping her hands on her slender flanks. 'I ought to be getting back, anyway. It's bound to be nearly teatime, and Aunt Grace probably wants me for something. There's so much to do—with the wedding.'

'So you are from the house. I wondered.' He gave her a meditative look. 'You're related to the Brothertons?'

'Yes, I'm Louise's cousin, Caroline Foxcroft. I'm going to be one of the bridesmaids. It's my very first time.'

There was an odd silence, then he said, 'Is it, indeed? Well, I'm Saul Kingsland, the honorary photographer.'

'Yes.' She flushed. 'I sort of guessed you were.' She paused. 'Won't they be wondering where you are?'

'I arrived a while ago, and got the introductions over. Then there seemed to be some problem with the florists, so I decided to be tactful, and take a look at the location.' Another brief silence. 'Did your cousin Louise tell you what I was planning?'

She nodded. 'A book—all about the wedding.' She smiled at him. 'We'll all be famous.'

He didn't return the smile. 'If it works. Maybe it isn't such a good idea, after all.'

'Oh, but you must do it. Louise—everyone— would be so disappointed if you didn't.'

'And that's all that matters, of course, at any wedding. Not to disappoint the bride.' His voice was dry. 'I'll have to try and remember that.' He paused. 'But I could always do a different kind of book. Children, maybe, with their pets, being happy as you were just now.'

'I'm not a child,' she said indignantly. 'I'm seventeen. I've got A-levels next year. And Reuben isn't mine. He belongs to Aunt Grace, really, only we both felt a bit in the way, so I brought him for a walk.'

'I'm sorry,' he said, but he looked more angry than regretful, she thought. 'But maybe it isn't such a bad thing to look younger than you are. When you're forty, you might be glad of it.' He glanced at his watch. 'Shall we still be in the way, do you think, or should we go back for tea now?'

'I expect so,' she said shyly. 'I'll have to take Reuben in the back way. Aunt Grace will be furious if I let him in the drawing-room in this state. I'll have to change, too,' she added, casting a stricken glance down at her bedraggled state.

'Well, don't take too long,' Saul Kingsland said. 'We outsiders have to stick together.' He held out his hand, and took her grubby fingers in his. 'Agreed?'

Words were suddenly impossible, so she nodded.

'Good. See you later, then.' At last he smiled at her, an easy, friendly grin which softened the rather saturnine lines of his face. Then, he turned and walked away along the bank.

Caroline took Reuben the other way, towards the gate which opened into the kitchen garden. She didn't hurry, and the dog frisked impatiently in front of her, running back constantly to see why she was taking so long.

Caroline was oblivious. Her mind was seething with a mass of confused impressions—half-remembered words and phrases. She thought of that final smile, and the clamour of her own heartbeat almost deafened her.

'Saul Kingsland,' she whispered. 'Saul Kingsland.'

And his name soared in her mind like some joyous, ecstatic song.

CHAPTER SIX

THE next time she saw him, at tea in the drawing-room, he was surrounded by other people, but he looked across at her, smiled and mouthed 'Hello', and Caroline felt a fresh burst of happiness explode inside her.

She was careful not to let it show. She melted into a corner of the window-seat, and took a cup of tea and a scone she did not want, for camouflage, and watched him from under her lashes, committing every feature, every gesture and turn of his head, every nuance in his voice to memory.

She was overwhelmed by what she felt for him, shaken by its swiftness and inevitability. Was this, she wondered helplessly, what people meant when they talked about love at first sight? And if so, why didn't they also mention how painful it could be when it was all on one side?

She watched Sue, Katie and the others moving round him, vying for his attention, and wished, for the first time in her life, that she could join in, that she had the confidence and experience to walk up to a man, and stake an unequivocal claim.

But, she hadn't, of course. And she wasn't so lost to all sense of reality as to dream he would welcome her advances. He was much older than she was, for one thing—at least twenty-eight, she thought. And he undoubtedly would have a girl-friend—no, a lover, she hastily amended, trying to

be sophisticated about it, although her face warmed
at the thought—even if she hadn't accompanied him
to Elmsleigh.

Leaning back against the warm window-panes,
Caroline gave herself up to a luxurious daydream
where she found herself walking once again by the
river with Saul. Felt his hand close round hers once
more. Heard him whisper, 'I thought I knew about
women, darling, but you're so young and sweet . . .'

'Caro, do pull yourself together, and help pass
the sandwiches round.' Susan's irritable voice returned her to earth with a bump. 'Honestly, you
look positively half-witted at times.'

And sometimes I feel it, Caroline thought,
guiltily, as she got to her feet. Because hankering
after Saul Kingsland has to be the stupidest thing
I've ever done. But luckily it's my secret, and that's
the way it's going to stay.

It wasn't a difficult resolve to maintain, as the
countdown to the wedding began, because, she soon
realised, he was totally absorbed in the job he'd
come there to do. And even though he was surrounded by pretty girls, all sending out unmistakable signals that they'd be in the market for an
enjoyable flirtation, or more, if he was willing, Saul
seemed immune to their overtures. But then, in his
profession, pretty girls were probably two a penny,
Caroline realised ruefully.

Watching him in action with a camera was a rev-
elation. He knew exactly what he wanted from them
all, and he cajoled and commanded until he got it.
Even Aunt Grace wasn't proof against his charm
when he chose to exert it.

Caroline wondered what they would do when the book came out. Watching Saul as closely as she did, she knew that as well as the deliberately posed shots, designed to present the idyllic façade of an English country wedding, there were dozens, in addition, of a far more candid and unflattering nature. Alongside the pretty pictures of people smiling in their best clothes, there would be other, franker illustrations of the inevitable strains, tensions and sheer bad humour that were an inevitable part of such an occasion.

She tried to visualise Aunt Grace's reaction when eventually she saw herself, red-faced and bristling, browbeating the men who had come to erect the marquee. Asked herself if Katie and Meg had realised Saul had even been there as they bickered endlessly over how the bridesmaids' hair should be arranged for the great day. Wondered how Louise and James would feel about the shot of themselves glaring at each other with sudden active dislike.

Clearly none of them shared her own sharp awareness of his every movement, she thought wryly. She'd hoped that Saul hadn't noticed her either, but she was wrong, because on the third morning he said abruptly, 'If you're going to continue to shadow me, you may as well make yourself useful—help with my gear—hand me things.'

'Oh, all right.' She tried to sound offhand, but inwardly she was transformed with delight.

It was, she thought afterwards, the happiest morning she'd ever spent. Saul was a hard taskmaster, frankly dictatorial and even abrasive if she was slow or clumsy in carrying out his commands, but she didn't care. Being with him as he worked, being able to call herself, inwardly, his assistant was pure joy.

At lunchtime, he said, 'Come on, let's get out of this hothouse atmosphere for a while. Get Reuben, and we'll walk down to the village.'

In the doorway of the local pub, he looked at her with sudden compunction. 'Hell, you're not old enough to drink, are you?'

'I am nearly.'

'Well, nearly isn't quite,' he said grimly. 'It's lemonade for you, my child.'

As he gave the order, Caroline wished rebelliously that she'd been old enough to say, 'Thank you, I'll have a frozen daiquiri.'

She had no idea what they were like, but she loved the sound of them. Not that the Crown would be likely to provide such delights, anyway. Mrs Ransome, the landlady, went in more for real ale and traditional meals.

She got her lemonade, mixed with orange juice and ice, and tinglingly cool and refreshing, and a wedge of Mrs Ransome's homemade steak and kidney pie to go with it.

'What are we going to do this afternoon?' she asked, as she scooped up the last gravy-rich crumbs.

There was a pause, then he said, 'I'm going to do some individual shots of the bridesmaids. I thought I might use the rose arbour, for some extra romanticism.'

'It should be sweet peas, really. That's what we're all meant to look like—all misty pinks and blues.' She sighed. 'My dress is mauve, which is my least favourite colour.'

'Well, I doubt whether I'll get round to you today.' He smiled at her swiftly. 'You're far too useful in other ways.'

'Then I don't mind waiting.' She glowed, bending to fuss the recumbent Reuben to mask her embarrassed pleasure.

'Would you like some ice-cream?' Saul studied the menu. 'There doesn't seem to be a great deal else in the way of dessert.'

'I shouldn't really have it,' she sighed.

'You can't be watching your weight.' His brows rose.

'No, my wretched skin,' she admitted. 'If I break out in spots at this late stage, Louise will kill me.'

'Is that likely to happen?'

'Well, it could. I usually get spots if I'm overexcited about something, and being a bridesmaid is the most marvellous thing that's ever happened to me.'

'I see.' Saul drank some of his beer. 'And what future thrills await you, Caroline Foxcroft? What's going to happen once you've taken your A-levels? What do you plan for your life?'

'I don't really know. I'm quite good at English, so I suppose I could teach.'

'You don't sound wildly enthusiastic about it,' he said drily.

'It's a worthwhile career,' she said primly.

'Who are you quoting?' He sent her a sardonic look.

'My headmistress.'

Her heart was beating suddenly, wildly and painfully. If this was a fairy-tale, she thought, he'd say,

'Forget teaching. You're too valuable to lose. Come and work for me instead.' If this was a fairy-tale.

As it was, he glanced at his watch. 'We'd better get back. I told the girls to sort out their favourite casual gear as well, so I could do some contrast shots.'

'Oh.' She looked down at herself. 'Will I do like this?'

'I've already done yours,' he said. 'Down on the riverbank with the dog that first day. Don't you remember?'

'Well, yes.' She tried not to feel disappointed. That day, she hadn't even known he was there, she thought. But at least he would photograph her properly once, even if it was in the grotty mauve dress.

I'll still go and change when we get back, she decided, in case he changes his mind.

She had some new white trousers which made the most of her slim hips and long legs, and a pretty French shirt in turquoise which tied at the midriff. She put up a hand and touched her hair. And maybe she could find something more exciting to do with this than the short, straight bob which they encouraged at her school. Katie had some heated rollers which she might be prepared to lend, she thought doubtfully.

But, when she got back to the house, she never had a chance to ask. Upstairs was chaos, with all the others trying to get ready at once.

'Katie!' Meg's voice sounded shocked and envious at the same time. 'You're not going to wear that for the informal photograph.'

Katie airily waved the minute black bikini she had just unearthed from her case. 'Saul said to wear things we felt comfortable in.' She giggled. 'Well, I can feel incredibly relaxed in this.'

Meg was just about to say something else when she spotted Caroline hesitating in the doorway. 'So there you are,' she said sharply. 'Your aunt has been looking everywhere for you. Where on earth have you been?'

'I've been helping Saul.'

'Don't you mean following him round like a stray puppy?' Katie's face was unamused as she glanced over her shoulder at the younger girl. 'But I'm afraid he'll have to dispense with your services this afternoon. Mrs Brotherton has a list of errands for you as long as her arm, and rather you than me,' she added waspishly.

'Oh.' Caroline's spirits plummeted. 'Did—did she mean right this minute?'

'Actually, I think she meant half an hour ago,' Katie said absently, holding the bikini up against herself, and studying her reflection. Her full lips curved in a catlike smile. 'Yes,' she said, half to herself, 'I think this will do very well.'

'Caroline.' Aunt Grace's tones floated magisterially up from the floor blow. 'Where is that girl?'

'She's here, Mrs Brotherton,' Katie called back, sending Caroline a malicious grin. 'Off you go, ducky, like a good little girl,' she added in an undertone.

Perhaps Aunt Grace won't want me for long, Caroline thought without much hope, as she trailed back downstairs.

But her hopes were dashed instantly. Her first task was to address a stack of envelopes enclosing thank-you notes from the bride and groom to people who had sent gifts. As James and Louise were known to be going to live in New Zealand, nearly everyone had sent money.

Caroline's hand was aching by the time she'd finished the pile in front of her. She wished that Aunt Grace wasn't such a stickler over personal letters being handwritten in every respect. I could have typed those envelopes in half the time, she thought forlornly.

As she got up to make her escape, Aunt Grace loomed again. 'Here are the stamps, Caroline. When you've attached them, you can take these and my other letters down to the post box in the village, and then go on to Mrs Everett's house with this note. She promised she would supply me with a list of the music she proposed to play before the arrival of the bride in church, but she hasn't done so.'

'Does it really matter?' Caroline's voice held a hint of rebellion. 'It's only something for people to listen to while they say rotten things about each other's hats.'

'We are talking of a sacred occasion, Caroline,' Aunt Grace said reprovingly. 'And Mrs Everett has an unfortunate habit of including secular music, even pop songs, I'm told, among her selections.'

'Heaven forbid,' Caroline muttered, *sotto voce*.

'So, you had better wait, and bring the list back with you,' Aunt Grace decreed, and sailed off again.

Caroline could have howled aloud. Her whole golden afternoon with Saul was slipping like sand through her fingers.

The sun was blazing down, and she felt hot, sticky and out of sorts by the time she reached Mrs Everett's. She found the parish organist on her dignity, and inclined to bridle when she heard Aunt Grace's request.

'Well, I remember Mrs Brotherton mentioning it, but I didn't really think she was serious. I've never had any complaints about my choice of music before, in all my years, and after all the fuss over the anthem I thought she might have been glad to leave it up to me.'

It took all Caroline's diplomacy to soothe her ruffled feathers and extract a grudging list from her.

'But I reserve the right to alter it,' was Mrs Everett's parting shot as Caroline began to trudge back to Elmsleigh.

Caroline stifled a groan. That was not the kind of message she wanted to pass on to her aunt in her present mood. But perhaps she could delay the evil hours, just for a while. After all, Aunt Grace wouldn't be expecting her back quite yet, she placated the unseen deity in charge of family obligations. So she could find Saul, apologise and explain, and hope against hope that he would still find something for her to do.

She chose the back way into the house yet again, and went round to the rose garden. The scent of the flowers hung heavy in the warm air, and bees drowsed among them. It was very quiet, and for a moment Caroline thought the photo session might be all over.

Then she heard Katie giggle, a small, soft sound that seemed, oddly, to have little to do with genuine amusement. There was something about it that halted Caroline dead in her tracks.

For a moment, she stood very still, an inward voice telling her it would be better—much better to return to the house. But something impelled her forward to the hedge of ancient shrub roses which protected the arbour.

Within its shelter was an oasis of green lawn with a moss-encrusted sundial as centrepiece. Katie was kneeling near the sundial, her hands tangled in her mane of blonde hair, lifting it away from her shoulders. The pose was totally, consciously provocative, and so was her smile.

She looked stunning, Caroline thought numbly, and incredibly sexy in that minimal black bikini.

'I feel like a Page Three girl,' Katie said, her voice warm and throaty. 'Do you think I look like one, Saul, darling?'

'You're rather overdressed.' Saul was putting another roll of film in the camera.

'Well, that's easily remedied,' Katie said softly. She put a hand behind her back to the clasp of her bikini top, and let the tiny garment fall to the grass. She arched her body slightly. 'How's that?'

'Spectacular.' There was amusement in his voice, and a faint huskiness too. 'Hold that.'

She obeyed, pouting. 'Do you think I could become a professional model?'

'It takes stamina. I'd stick to amateur status, if I were you.'

'You really don't take me seriously, do you?'

'I certainly don't underestimate you,' Saul said, after a pause. 'Turn slightly. Look at me over your shoulder. That's good—that's fantastic.'

'Well, do you realise just how much ma-noeuvring it's taken to be alone with you like this?' Katie's voice was throaty and seductive.

'The manipulations haven't been totally one-sided.' Saul sounded faintly abstracted, but his words made Caroline's hands ball into taut, painful fists at her sides. 'I managed to deal with the others in record time, so that I could devote the rest of the afternoon to you.'

'I'm thankful to hear it,' Katie said, laughing. She paused. 'Of course, the hardest job has been getting rid of the faithful puppy constantly trailing behind you. Honestly, Saul, why do you encourage that grotesque-looking child to hang around you all the time?'

There was a silence. In spite of the heat, Caroline felt cold sweat breaking out on her forehead. Suddenly, she wanted to run, but her feet seemed rooted to the spot, holding her there captive and hu-miliated, waiting, without breathing, for his reply.

He said slowly, his words dropping like stones into Caroline's frantic silence. 'I suppose I'm sorry for her. For goodness' sake, she's practically an object lesson in how not to look!'

'Well, what do you think it's like for us, being saddled with her as the sixth bridesmaid?' Katie demanded pettishly. 'It's like taking part in some freak show.'

'As a matter of interest, exactly why was she chosen?'

Katie shrugged, her pert breasts bouncing. 'A case of needs must, apparently. Louise wanted Susan, but the family decreed that if she had the pretty cousin, she had to ask the ugly one too. We all prayed she'd refuse, but she didn't, of course, and James and Louise were absolutely furious. She's like a fish out of water, being so much younger. And I swear that nose of hers grows longer every day.'

'Well, she's given me one devil of a problem.' Saul's voice was angry. 'How the hell can I camouflage her—hide her away among the rest of you in the wedding groups tomorrow? Her height's against her, for one thing. She'll stick out like a sore thumb. I can leave her out of the book, except in the most marginal way perhaps, but I can't cut her out of the official photographs.'

Katie giggled. 'You're the professional, darling. Can't you arrange some convenient slip of the camera? I'm sure Louise would be eternally grateful, not to mention the rest of us.'

'Well, I'll have to do something.' Saul's tone was short. 'But she's my problem, not yours. Now, lean back on the grass. Draw up one leg slightly. That's good—that's amazing.'

'Is it enough?' Katie allowed one hand to toy almost idly with the strings which fastened her bikini briefs at the hip.

'That has to be your decision.' The amusement was back in his voice.

Katie pouted. 'You could—help me make up my mind.' She paused. 'These damned strings seem to have knotted.'

'How incredibly inconvenient of them.' Saul walked across the grass and dropped to one knee beside her. 'Let me see.' His hand moved, and the little black triangle of material joined its counterpart on the grass. 'There,' he said softly. 'It was really quite—simple, after all.'

Caroline heard Katie giggle again, and saw her arms go up to wind round Saul's neck and draw him down to her. The stark knowledge of what she was going to witness was enough, at least, to release her from the almost catatonic trance imprisoning her there.

She took a step backwards, slowly, quietly, terrified of revealing her presence. Then another. And another, placing each foot like an automaton. Backing away across the expanse of the garden with infinite, heart-rending care. Her hands were clenched into fists at her sides, her nails scoring the soft palms. She wanted to lift them, to cover her eyes, to block her ears, to press against her parted lips, and dam back the sounds of the pain which was beginning to tear her apart, and which she could not utter.

She shuddered, feeling the ground dip and lurch beneath her feet.

She thought—I'm going to faint. But I can't. Not here. Not now. I have to keep going. Have to.

She stood still for a moment, breathing deeply, forcing the swirling world to steady itself. Then, when at last she was sure she was at sufficient distance from the rose arbour for her retreat to be unseen and unheard by its occupants, she turned tail and ran like some small, frightened animal for the sanctuary of the house.

She just made it into the cloakroom leading off the hall. She hung over the basin, retching miserably, her whole being one silent moan of agony.

From some far distance, she heard approaching feet.

'Caroline?' Aunt Grace's voice was shocked. 'Whatever is the matter with you? Your parents have just arrived. I wanted you to show them to their room.'

She tried to speak, to form coherent words, but the world was spinning again crazily, out of control, and she let herself slide down into the merciful, encompassing darkness.

Aunt Grace's anger when she learned that her younger niece intended to return home, and take no further part in the wedding, was formidable indeed. At any other time, Caroline would have been totally cowed by it.

But not then, or, in fact, ever again, Carly thought, looking back over the years with a wry smile.

On that nightmare afternoon there was no threat, no browbeating or level of icy displeasure which could make the slightest impression on her decision. For the first time in her life, she was adamant, simply repeating over and over again that she was ill—too sick to be a bridesmaid, and had to go home at once. And eventually Aunt Grace had, furiously, given way, at the same time making it clear that this defection would not be forgiven or forgotten in a hurry.

The journey home was a rapid one. She lay on the back seat of the car, propped up with cushions, pretending to be asleep while her parents conversed in low, worried tones about her pallor.

The doctor, hastily summoned, and rushed off his feet with cases of summer flu, gave her a cursory examination, pronounced her another victim, and left some antibiotics which Caroline flushed down the toilet as soon as she was alone.

She had little difficulty in persuading her parents that a couple of days in bed was all she needed, and that they could return to Elmsleigh and enjoy the rest of the wedding without her.

Once they'd departed, she locked her door against the housekeeper's kindly concern and offers of cool drinks and nourishing snacks and gave way to the agony of misery inside her.

She wept until there were no more tears left, then lay, harsh sobs still tearing at her chest, staring into space.

She'd always known that Susan was the pretty one, and she'd accepted this without resentment. But that was before she had been taught in one cruel, devastating lesson just how ugly, how unlovable she really was.

Saul's words jarred her mind, seemed to sear their way into her wincing brain.

An object lesson in how not to look.

How could he? she moaned, grinding her clenched fists against her teeth. Oh, how could he be so unkind?

All those hours she'd spent with him, delighting in his company. Eagerly treasuring every look, every smile, her confidence in her burgeoning womanhood blossoming every minute—each one had been a lie, a total betrayal.

Because Saul Kingsland—her friend—her first love—didn't even like her. He pitied her, and that was bad enough. In fact, it was the worst thing that had ever happened to her. But he also found her an embarrassment, not just personally, but professionally, and that was even more terrible.

She was too plain—too gawky—too hideous to be photographed. She was a freak—a monster. That was what they all thought, talking and laughing about her behind her back.

In a way, it didn't matter what James and Louise thought. She supposed that she knew, subconsciously, why they'd asked her to be a bridesmaid. It didn't matter what any of them said about her— except Saul—only Saul.

Fresh pain lashed at her, and she moaned, wrapping her arms defensively round her body. She knew—she'd always known that eavesdroppers never heard any good about themselves, so why had she gone on standing there, listening, letting herself be wounded like that?

Because she'd been waiting—praying for Saul to defend her, she thought, wincing. She'd naïvely expected him to be angry at Katie's poisoned remarks—to contradict her—slap her down. But instead—instead...

She sank her teeth into her lower lip until she tasted blood. Every hope, every innocent fantasy had been shattered and there was nothing left. No dreams. Only the harsh reality of knowing herself unwanted, and a laughing-stock.

Only the memory of seeing Katie naked and willing in Saul's arms. And that was the greatest betrayal of all.

She kept her door locked and didn't emerge for over twenty-four hours. She didn't want to see anyone—face anyone, even her family when they got back from the wedding. The thought that perhaps their affection was a mask for secret pity was more than she could bear. Maybe even her closest friends at school felt sorry for her too, or perhaps she was the butt for their careless cruelty behind her back.

She shivered. It would be easy to stay shut up here. She could understand for the first time why people cut themselves off from the world—became reclusive. If it meant avoiding the kind of hurt she'd experienced, then it could almost be worth it, she realised with anguish.

I'll never be able to meet anyone again, she thought. Never be able to look them in the eye without wondering if they're laughing at me, saying things about me. I can't bear it—I can't . . .

She felt a scream rising inside her, and bit it back. She felt as if she was going mad. She wasn't even eighteen yet, and she was contemplating becoming some kind of hermit.

And Saul Kingsland had done this to her. She'd loved him. She'd trusted him and he'd destroyed her, she thought, and felt the misery inside her beginning to harden into anger and bitterness. Somehow she would make him pay for what he'd done. She would make him suffer as badly as she was hurting now.

She said aloud, 'I will destroy him,' and heard the words echo in the lonely silence.

All she had to do was find the way.

She spent a lot of her solitary vigil in front of her dressing-table mirror, examining herself minutely, carrying out the most complete and candid self-appraisal of her life.

By the time it was over, she knew what she was going to do.

'So there you are,' was Sue's greeting, when at last Caroline went downstairs. Her sister was reclining on the drawing-room sofa, flicking through a magazine. 'What a little idiot you are, letting everyone down like that.' She preened slightly. 'As it was, Louise asked me to be chief bridesmaid, and Megs and Katie weren't altogether pleased, I can tell you.' She giggled. 'In fact, it wasn't Katie's day at all. It seems Saul Kingsland cleared off back to London and didn't ask for her phone number. She was livid. But it serves her right. She was playing with fire, getting involved with him in the first place.' She paused. 'Are you all right, Caro? You've gone positively green.'

'I'm fine,' Caroline said quietly.

Sue yawned. 'Well, I'll take your word for it. You've got the most amazing shadows under your eyes,' she added critically. 'Are you sure you should be out of bed? You've got to be fit to go back to school.'

'I'm not going back.'

Sue gaped at her. 'What nonsense is this? Of course you are. You've got important exams coming up.'

Caroline shrugged. 'They're no longer important to me.'

Sue sat up. 'But what are you going to do instead?'

'Find myself work.'

'Well, heaven knows what kind of job you'll get with no qualifications,' Sue said with asperity. 'Honestly, Caro, you're the family bluestocking. You can't let us down like this.'

'Perhaps I want to change my image.'

'And maybe it isn't that easy.' Sue's gaze was frankly disbelieving. 'What in the world's come over you, Caro? Have you told Mother and Father what you're contemplating?'

'Not yet.'

'Then let's hope they can make you see sense. You had a career all planned.'

'I had one planned for me, certainly,' Caroline retorted. 'Now I'm thinking of a future instead. And not as a spinster schoolmarm, either.'

'And just how do you intend to begin?'

Caroline pushed her glasses up her nose. 'With cosmetic surgery,' she said, and walked out of the room.

And I did, Carly thought, remembering the long, painful and expensive months which had followed. She'd used part of her godmother's legacy to have her nose shortened, and her teeth straightened and capped. She'd had the shape of her chin fractionally altered, and learned to use contact lenses instead of her glasses. She'd joined a modelling school, and learned how to walk and stand and use her brand-new face and body for the camera. She'd still been a student when Clive had spotted her.

Since which, she hadn't looked back. And, if being a success had been all she'd wanted, then she would have been both happy and fulfilled.

Yet she had never let herself forget why she was doing this. Each time she looked in the mirror, she thought of Saul Kingsland, and promised herself that one day—one day they would meet again. She knew the opportunity would arise, and all she had to do was be patient. After all, natural justice demanded that she should be given the chance to ruin his life as surely as he'd ruined hers.

He'd destroyed the real Caroline Foxcroft, and replaced her with Carly North, the western world's most synthetic creation. An artefact who belonged nowhere, and was accepted by no one.

A plastic doll, she thought with contempt, who knew how to make the camera love her.

And a doll about to turn on her unwitting creator.

She laughed, and heard the sound splinter bleakly into a sob in the stillness of the room.

CHAPTER SEVEN

As THE bow of the caique cut through the water, Carly felt the cool misting of spray on her face, and drew a sharp breath of exhilaration.

Behind her, she could hear laughter, and the chink of glasses. Adonis, the boat's skipper, had produced a bottle of ouzo for the film crew and was pouring with a lavish hand.

She'd smilingly refused the offer of a drink. She needed to keep a cool head. She couldn't afford to be careless—to allow anything to go wrong now, at this stage in the game.

In the three weeks leading up to their departure for Thyrsos, Saul had been in constant touch with her. He'd been at her side when she'd signed the contract which bound her for a year to the exclusive promotion of Flawless cosmetics, and he was there, fending off awkward or too personal questions at the inevitable Press conferences which followed the announcement of the Flawless Girl's identity.

'You had the choice of every model in the UK,' a reporter asked Saul. 'So, why this particular girl?'

'You must be blind to ask a question like that,' Saul drawled. 'Miss North is an incredibly beautiful girl, and an angel in front of the camera— an absolute natural. As soon as I saw her, I knew she had to be my first and only choice.'

109

Carly forced herself to smile at his words, but under the shelter of the table they were seated at her hands clenched together in her lap until the knuckles turned white.

She wanted to scream aloud, But it wasn't always like that. When I was Caroline Foxcroft, I was too ugly—too grotesque to feature in his work. He rejected me totally.

Why don't I say it? she thought, the pain of it wrenching her apart. Why don't I finish it now— before it goes too far—before I'm in too deep?

And then, standing at the back, she saw Mark Clayfield. Their eyes met, and he smiled faintly, inclining his head. Carly looked away swiftly, her pulses thumping.

No, she thought. She had chosen what she was going to do, and she would see it through to the bitter end.

The tabloids the following day were full of gloating stories about ' ''My One and Only,'' says playboy Saul', their columns listing the glamorous women he'd escorted on both sides of the Atlantic, commenting on the fact that he'd been lured back across the Atlantic to spearhead the Flawless campaign, and speculating openly about his relationship with Carly.

Carly reacted furiously when she read the more lurid pieces. Nor was her temper improved by Saul's amused acceptance of the gossip and innuendo which permeated most of the stories.

'Money and sex,' he told her succinctly. 'That's what sells newspapers. And although no actual figures are available, everyone knows that the Flawless campaign is going to be the most expensive cosmetics launch ever. So they can say we're not only being paid vast sums, but are heavily involved with each other as well. Rather like having your cake and eating it.'

'Don't you care what they say?' she asked hotly.

He shrugged. 'Why should I?' The look he sent her was faintly edged. 'We both know how far from the truth those stories are.'

Carly bit her lip and turned away.

Since that night at her flat when she'd come so perilously near to surrender, she had been ultra-careful where Saul was concerned.

Not, she was forced to admit, that it had been totally necessary. Although she saw him so often, there had been no further attempt on his part to make their relationship a sexual one. And, if she was completely honest, the last occasion hadn't been his fault.

I did throw myself at him, she reminded herself ruefully. And after that the situation—snowballed.

But she had not made that mistake again, and Saul himself seemed content to let the situation develop at the pace she dictated. When he greeted her, or said goodbye, he invariably kissed her, but more often than not it was a light touch on her cheek. When he kissed her mouth, she was aware that he was holding himself rigidly in check, allowing his lips merely to brush her own.

So far, it was all going to plan. She wanted him hungry, his entire attention focused exclusively on herself.

And he was being clever about it too, letting her see that, although he might be starving for her, he was capable of keeping his appetite within bounds.

He thought, of course, that patience and for-
bearance were all that he needed. That sooner or
later her own needs, her own sexual curiosity, would
drive her into his arms.

He believed, she had come to realise, that they
would be lovers on Thyrsos. And now they were
almost there at the island.

She heard a step behind her on deck, and tensed
involuntarily, knowing who it would be. Filming
for the campaign had started in earnest almost as
soon as the ink was dry on the contract. She had
found herself whisked from one location to
another, from a château in the Loire valley to the
grounds of an English stately home, where a small
Georgian gazebo overlooked a lake afloat with
water-lilies.

The emphasis of the campaign, as Septimus
Creed had made clear, was sheer romanticism, designed to appeal to every woman's secret dreams.
And at any other time Carly would have revelled
in the exquisite costumes chosen for her, appreciated the care that had selected the elegant
background for each commercial, and enjoyed the
professionalism of the director and film crew.

As it was, the knowledge of what she was about
to do haunted her. Her nights were plagued by
troubled dreams, and she awoke more than once to
find tears on her face.

And, whenever and wherever the shooting was
taking place, Saul was always there, a yard or so
behind the camera, watching every movement and
every expression, his eyes never leaving her.

He had taken numerous shots of her already, but the major part of his work on the campaign would be completed on Thyrsos.

Everything, Carly thought, would come to completion on Thyrsos.

As Saul's hands descended on her shoulders, his fingers warm and strong through the flimsy Indian cotton top she was wearing, she forced herself to relax, to lean back against him.

'Adonis says we'll be there in half an hour.'

She flung a smile over her shoulder at him. 'British time or Greek time?'

'Does it matter?'

'Not at all,' she said. Although it might, she thought, in the not too distant future, when I want to make a swift getaway. 'It's a wonderful day for a sea trip.' She paused. 'I'm testing the Flawless sunblock cream.'

'I hope you've brought plenty,' he said wryly. 'Sunbathing is definitely out while we're shooting. We can't handle a piebald model.'

'I could always go for an all-over tan,' she said lightly, and felt his fingers tighten on her shoulders in response.

He thought that was a signal, she thought with satisfaction. What was the phrase he'd once used to her? 'A declaration of intent.' Well, he would find out how wrong he was.

'Once work is finished, we might be able to steal some time to ourselves—maybe spend a few days on Mykonos,' Saul said softly into her ear. 'Did you like Mykonos?'

She shrugged. 'I liked what I saw on the way from the airport to the boat.'

'That's not giving the place a chance. It's beautiful, and it can be a little crazy. I'd like to show it to you. May I?'

'Maybe.' She made the word husky with anticipation.

After all, she thought, the more she promised, the more devastated he would be when she brought the world crashing down around him. And that was now only a matter of time.

She suppressed a shiver. She'd waited so long for this, manipulating events to her own ends, and now, suddenly, she had the feeling that she was no longer in control of circumstances—that she was being swept along by a current, too strong and too malignant for her to restrain. That there was now an inevitability about events which frightened her.

I must be weakening, she thought in self-derision. I've let his kisses get to me.

It was all part of life's unfairness—that, in spite of everything, Saul Kingsland's lightest touch on her hand had the power to stir her to her soul. But at least it meant she did not have to pretend—to fake a response when he came close to her—held her—because intuition told her that Saul was too worldly, and too experienced not to know.

Everything has to be paid for, she thought, even vengeance. And perhaps this harsh torment of yearning which Saul awoke in her was the price to be exacted from her in frustration, bitterness and tears.

Septimus Creed was waiting on the small stone jetty as Adonis manoeuvred the craft to its moorings.

'Welcome to Thyrsos,' he called. He summoned forward a stocky, smiling man in an immaculate white coat. 'This is Kostas, who'll be looking after us at the villa with his wife Penelope. If you can get your luggage ashore, Kostas will have it brought up to the house by donkey. In the meantime, we climb up these steps. I suggest you take them by degrees until you get acclimatised.'

The steps were steep, bordered by a low wall to the seaward side, and rough, as if they'd been hewn out of the tall cliff-face itself.

As they probably had, Carly thought, as she started up them. She soon outstripped the film crew, whom she could hear grumbling and cursing good-naturedly behind her, but she was aware of Saul at her shoulder, keeping pace with her easily, no matter how fast she climbed.

His voice reached her laconically. 'If this is a race, what's the prize?'

'Wait and see,' she tossed back at him.

'In that case——' Saul said, and overtook her easily, his long legs carrying him further and further ahead.

The first mad impetus which had taken her up the steps at a gallop was beginning to subside. It had been cool on the water, but here on land the sun seemed to beat down on her unprotected head, its heat reflected back off the cliff's bleached rock.

She thought, I should never have started this.

But the impulse to run had been too great. She'd been confined for too long, on the plane, in the car, and finally on the boat, with Saul never more than a few feet away from her. The word 'escape' had been drumming in her mind, and as soon as she felt solid ground under her feet she'd just taken off.

She paused for a moment, her hands pressed to her waist. A lizard lay on the wall beside her, its colour blending with the dusty parched stones, its only sign of life the swift, rhythmic panting which distended its small sides.

She said aloud, trying to catch her breath, 'I know how you feel,' and the little creature vanished in a blur of movement.

Saul was waiting for her at the top of the steps, where a huge terrace had been built overlooking the sea. Pride made her take the last few steps two at a time.

He said, 'Why all the hurry? Thyrsos is a small island. There's nowhere to run to...'

She stared at him for a dazed moment. It was as if he was warning her—as if he knew. *Nowhere to run to.* She swallowed. But that was nonsense. Saul knew—suspected nothing. How could he? And there was always somewhere to run—some escape— some refuge. Always.

He added, 'Unless, of course, you were rushing to see this.'

He took her by the shoulders, and turned her to face the bay and the horizon.

Carly caught her breath. The sea was a myriad of colours from amethyst to turquoise, crested here and there with tiny caps of white foam. In the distance she could see an island, and another beyond it, both fringed in green, the grey of their rocky interiors deepening to mauve in the intense light.

'Oh, how beautiful.'

'Flawless,' Saul agreed, an odd note in his voice.

She glanced at him, standing beside her, and realised he was looking not at the view but at herself,
his eyes brooding and intent. For a moment his gaze
held hers, then it shifted, sweeping down her body
from the small, high breasts, frankly outlined
against her thin top by the flurry of her breathing,
to her pink-tipped toes in the rope-soled sandals,
and then back to her parted lips.

He said, quietly, 'I claim my prize,' and took a
step towards her, cancelling the small space which
separated them.

A shaft of pure sensation pierced her, clenching
her inner muscles like a fist. It was so painful and
so sweet that she wanted to cry out, but no sound
came from her dry throat. She was trembling
suddenly, in anticipation and need, and she lifted
a hand, pushing her sunglasses further up the bridge
of her small nose in the small, nervous gesture she
hadn't used for years.

And saw him stop, the dark face suddenly
puzzled, his brows snapping together in concentration as if he was trying to recapture some elusive
memory.

Sudden panic assailed her. If he thought hard
enough, he might just recall the gauche, plain
adolescent who'd created that silly, restless little
movement. And she couldn't let him do that. She
had to stop him thinking...

She made herself move, step forward towards
him, so that their bodies were almost touching.
Made herself smile, the tip of her tongue flicking
along her lower lip. Made herself whisper, 'I'm glad
you won,' as her hands reached up to his shoulders.

Immediately, Saul's arms went round her, drawing her fully against him in a way he had not allowed himself to do since that night at her flat. The sharp, arrested look went from his face, to be replaced with the starkness of a desire he could no longer conceal. For a long moment, he held her against the aroused warmth of his body, as if he was imprinting her on his flesh for all eternity, then he bent his head, and his mouth took hers.

She couldn't resist—couldn't push him away, after the explicit invitation of her words and actions. She would have to endure it—somehow.

But mere endurance was impossible. As Saul's lips parted her own, and she felt the thrust of his tongue against hers, her whole body was invaded by a startling, melting sweetness.

She thought frantically, This is dangerous, I can't let it happen. And she tried to retreat from him by sheer effort of will. But it was too late. Control was giving way to imperative instinct.

As Saul's kiss deepened inexorably, Carly found she was pressing her body against his, her breasts aching against the hard wall of his chest, her hips grinding slowly and languorously against his own. The sun was all around her, scorching her to her bones, dazzling her. Its heat was inside her too, burning her up, but Saul's mouth on hers was cool, like the first rainfall on some desert, and she drank from his lips, from his tongue, as if they were her sole salvation.

'*I want you.*' They were his words, breathed against her parted, eager lips, but they could have been her own, because they were there, unbidden, in her mind, struggling for utterance. And that was not just danger, but madness...

The cough, quiet, apologetic but definite, separated them. A woman had emerged on to the terrace, and was standing, her black eyes sparkling with interest and amusement, waiting for their attention. She wore a dark dress covered by a spotless white apron, and held a list.

'*Me sinkhorite*. I ask your pardon.' She looked at the list. 'Who are you, please?'

'My name is Kingsland.' Saul's voice was ragged as he sought to control his breathing. 'And this is Kyria North.'

'I am Penelope, me.' Her smile was broad and welcoming. 'Come with me, please, and I will show you where you will sleep.'

Carly wasn't sure that she could move—that her legs would support her. Only a kiss, she thought feverishly, yet her pulse-beats were deafening her, and every inch of her body was quiveringly awakened.

'Are you all right?' Saul was staring at her, his face suddenly concerned.

She took a breath. 'Sep Creed was right.' She managed, somehow, to sound rueful, even amused. 'I should never have tried to run up those steps in this heat.'

'Let me help you.' Before she could protest, Saul had lifted her deftly into his arms, as if she was a child. 'Lead on,' he told Penelope.

She gave them an arch look, then, with a murmured, '*Po po po,*' she took them round the side of the villa to where a flight of steps, almost masked by flowering vine, led to the upper floor.

'Your own entrance,' she announced beaming. 'Only your rooms are here.'

Carly felt herself swallow as Saul carried her with seeming effortlessness up the steps. Events—the whole situation seemed to be out of her control. Certainly, she hadn't bargained for this—neither for the isolation, nor the proximity of their rooms, and the intimacy this implied.

Both rooms, she saw with alarm, had sliding glass doors which gave on to a joint balcony. There wasn't any kind of dividing wall or screen to give even an illusion of privacy between them.

Her room was cool and shadowy after the glare of the sun. The floor was tiled in marble, and the walls were covered in a pale blue wash. The furnishings were simple enough—a cupboard for clothes, a chest of drawers in some dark wood, and a wide bed invitingly made up with plump pillows and snowy sheets—and never in this world intended for single occupation, Carly thought numbly.

Saul put her down in the middle of the bed. He was very gentle, but his hands lingered on her, and she had to resist an impulse to cower away.

'You like, *ne*?' Penelope glanced around her with evident satisfaction. 'There is one bathroom only, which you share.' She gave them a droll look. 'But no problem, maybe.'

Carly's hands clenched at her sides. She could foresee all kinds of difficulties . . .

'Everything's fine.' Saul smiled at the housekeeper. 'And you are the wife of Kostas. Have you worked here long?'

She nodded emphatically. 'Since Kyrios Athol first built this house. He is a good man, and I like to welcome his friends.' She paused. 'I am also the sister of Adonis, who brought you in the boat. And my other brother, Yannis, has a good taverna in the village, by the edge of the harbour. There he cooks the swordfish which he catches himself.'

'Then, we'll be sure to pay him a visit, won't we, darling?' Saul looked down at Carly. 'Swordfish is a favourite of mine.'

She moistened her lips with the tip of her tongue. 'I—I don't think I've ever tasted it.'

'Then you've a treat in store.' He paused. 'Now, take it easy until dinner. Sep Creed's calling a short briefing meeting after the meal, but until then our time's our own.'

He gave her a swift smile, then followed Penelope out of the room.

Carly lay back against the pillows. Her breathing was beginning to return to its normal pace, and her inner weakness was dissipating. But there was no real reassurance to be gained from this. It was only a temporary respite, she thought feverishly, wrapping her arms round her body.

How could her body respond so wantonly, drowning in sensation, to a man her mind hated and rejected? she asked herself with a kind of despair. What was wrong with her?

This is what you planned, said a small, cold voice in her brain. You wanted him in your net—caught—trapped—obsessed by you here on Thyrsos. Well, you have your wish. Only, traps can sometimes be double-edged.

She shivered. There was one commercial to shoot with the film crew, then they would be returning to Britain, and she and Saul would be working virtually alone together.

She was geared for that. She'd rehearsed the role she would play, driving him slowly crazy in the sunlight.

But all her ploys were daytime ones. She hadn't reckoned on the fact that he would be spending his nights only a few paces away from her.

'Nowhere to run to.' The words returned to torment her, and she rolled over, pressing her hands to her ears.

Not long to go, she told herself. You can't weaken—chicken out now. You started this. You have to finish it.

But the truth was, she hadn't realised how many other people would be involved—hadn't stopped to think how far-reaching the repercussions of her private vengeance might be.

She'd forgotten her own innate professionalism which had responded joyously to the demands made on her during the filming of the commercials. It had been hard work, but fun, too, and a real camaraderie had built up among them all. And the commercials were undoubtedly some of the best work she'd ever done. The director and Sep Creed had worn smiles of quiet satisfaction at the end of each day's shooting.

Yet all that time, all that money, all that artistic and creative effort was going to be totally wasted, she thought with regret.

What she was about to do would never be forgotten or forgiven. She had to make up her mind to that. She was facing the deliberate sacrifice of her career.

Goodbye, Carly North, she thought with a tinge of sadness. You served your purpose. Now you can vanish back into well-deserved obscurity, and Caroline Foxcroft can take over again.

She was aware of a strange, panicky sensation in the pit of her stomach. Was it possible for her to do that—to wipe out the new face, the new persona she'd created for herself? Or would she find herself for the rest of her life caught in a kind of limbo between the two identities?

She moved restlessly, pressing her face into the pillow.

Pull yourself together, she adjured herself impatiently. You're just tired after the flight.

She would sleep for a while. Then, after a shower, she would be ready to face the final battle in her secret war against Saul Kingsland. She dealt with her contact lenses, then lay back, closing her eyes, emptying her mind quite deliberately, letting the warmth and her weariness have their way with her.

But there was no immediate peace to be found. Saul's face seemed to burn against the inside of her eyelids, his presence as real as if he'd been actually there in the room, bending over the bed, his hands reaching down for her...

She sat bolt upright with a little cry, staring round her. But she was alone. Only the shadows were there, deeper than they had been. Peering at her watch, Carly saw with astonishment that she'd actually been asleep for two hours.

Had she really dreamed about Saul all that time? she asked herself, her heart thudding uncomfortably. Surely not? Dreams were odd, stretching a few seconds into what could seem a lifetime. There would have been other fantasies, other recollections in her mind, but her subconscious was playing tricks on her, submerging them beneath an all-pervading vision of Saul.

She became aware of other things—the sound of voices in the distance, the rustle of leaves on the balcony as the evening breeze quickened, the splash of water closer at hand.

Saul, it seemed, had beaten her to that shower. She found it a disturbing thought, and for a moment an image assailed her, unbidden but potent, of his body, lean, tanned and wearing nothing but a few drops of water.

She dismissed it instantly and angrily, conscious that her skin had warmed involuntarily, as if she'd entered the bathroom without thinking, and found him there, in reality, naked.

Carly bit her lip. She could only hope that, when it was her turn, there would be at least a bolt on the communicating door with his room that she could use.

Someone, she saw, had brought in her case while she was asleep, and she would be far better employed unpacking something to wear for dinner than indulging in—ridiculous erotic fantasies.

Impatient with herself, she reached for her contact lens case, and began the familiar routine. But, as she positioned the first lens on her fingertip and raised it towards her eye, a stronger than usual gust of air from the open window lifted the tiny, transparent disc and flicked it into infinity.

'Oh, no!' Carly wailed. 'I don't believe it.'

She remained totally still, peering down at herself, praying that the errant lens had blown down on to her lap, and was trapped in a fold of her clothing, but there seemed no sign of it.

She said again, 'Oh, no,' and scrambled off the bed, trying to cause as little disarrangement of its covering as possible.

She had a spare pair, of course, but they were in the bathroom cupboard in her London flat. And tucked away inside her suitcase were the despised glasses which she'd promised herself she would only ever use in the direst emergency. She flung herself at the case and began to tug at its strap.

From the bathroom doorway, Saul said, 'Is something wrong?'

He was leaning there, very much at his ease. One brief, shaken glance told her that the water had darkened his hair to the colour of midnight, and the towel he wore draped round his hips did little more than preserve the decencies. That swift fantasy of a few moments ago had only told half the story, she realised, feeling the betraying colour surge into her face, and hating herself for it.

She said shortly, 'Everything's fine.'

He shrugged. 'Then I apologise for intruding. I thought I heard you call out.'

He was already turning away when she said reluctantly, 'As a matter of fact, there is something. I—I've let my contact lens blow away. And...'

'And you can't see well enough without it to find it,' he supplied drily. 'I get the idea.'

He walked across the room, slowly and carefully, staring down at the mottled tiles.

'This bloody floor doesn't help,' he commented. 'You've no notion which direction...? No, of course you haven't.' He went down on one knee and began a minute examination of the floor round the bed. 'What we really need is a miracle, but in case there isn't one, how much of a problem is this going to be for you? I mean, how much can you see without them?'

'Not enough.' She had her spectacle case in her hand now. Saul would soon be wondering why she didn't do the obvious thing—put on her glasses and join him in the search.

But, after her previous slip with her sunglasses, she dared not risk it. The colour and shape of the frames were too reminiscent of those she'd worn as a girl. She'd jogged his memory once. Twice might be too often.

He said, 'So how many more secrets have you for me to discover?'

Tension gripped her. 'I—don't understand.'

'I usually notice things like lenses, but with you I didn't.' He sounded rueful. 'Shows how hard I find it to be objective about you.'

Her flush deepened hectically. 'I—forget I wear them half the time. I feel so stupid—letting one blow away like this.'

'I always understood that was a natural hazard of the things.' Saul paused abruptly, and leaned forward, frowning. He said softly, 'Good lord! Wonder of wonders, I do believe...' He gave her a swift grin. 'Hold your breath, sweetheart. I think I've found it. Pass me a tissue.'

'Oh!' Carly sighed in gratitude and relief. 'Oh, I don't know how to thank you!'

Saul's smile became faintly oblique. He said quite gently, 'I could suggest any variety of ways,' and put the lens, safe in a fold of tissue, in her outstretched hand.

A sudden silence descended—pressed on them, closed them in together. He was so close to her that she could even see the faint dampness lingering on his chest hair—smell the scent of the soap he'd used. It would be so easy to reach out to him again— offer her lips. So easy, and so fatal.

She swallowed, dry-mouthed, desperately aware that she must break the tense expectancy of the moment. 'You—you said—no pressure.'

He said, 'And I meant it, heaven help me.' He got lithely to his feet, adjusting his towel as he did so. He looked at her levelly. 'But my patience has limits, and I'm fast reaching them.'

Her voice shook. 'You make that sound like a threat.'

Saul shook his head. 'No,' he said. 'Only a warning.' His smile was brief, almost impersonal, then he turned and walked away, back to his own room.

For a long moment, Carly stayed where she was, on her knees, staring after him. Then, slowly, the rigidity dissolved from her slim body, and she began to tremble.

CHAPTER EIGHT

THE three remaining columns of the little temple reared in apricot splendour against the azure of the morning sky.

Carly waited in the shade of an olive tree for the director to signal the start of the take. It was simple enough. They'd shot the close-ups already, the camera lingering lovingly on every plane and contour of her face, highlighted by the Flawless cosmetics.

Now all she had to do was walk slowly across the crumbling slabs of the pavement, and stand with her hand resting against one of the columns, looking down at the sea.

She reached down and smoothed the folds of the filmy white dress she was wearing. It had been designed on the lines of a Greek *chiton* and had a graceful simplicity that lent itself perfectly to its surroundings.

Her hair had been wound into a smooth coil and pinned on top of her head, with one long curl allowed to hang down over the shoulder her dress left bare.

It was much the same style as the one she'd worn to the Flawless reception, she thought. That was the night which had begun it all—when she'd made her quest for vengeance into a reality. And now, here on this small and sunlit island, it would finally reach its culmination.

The breeze came snaking across the small plateau carved out of the stark hillside where they stood, and Carly shivered slightly as she glanced towards the temple ruins. No one seemed to know to which of the ancient Greek deities the little sanctuary had been dedicated.

Maybe, she thought, it could even be Nemesis, the dark goddess of retribution herself.

She leaned back, feeling the roughness of the tree's bark beneath her fingers, staring up through the rustling silver leaves towards the sky.

The past week had been easier to cope with than she could have hoped for. She had worked with the film crew early each morning before the real heat of the day began, and afterwards they'd all stayed together as a team, enjoying the small sand and shingle beaches near the villa, or lounging beside its swimming pool.

Saul had not always joined them. He'd rented a motorbike in town, and gone on a photographic exploration of the island. He'd suggested once, casually, that she should accompany him, but had applied no further pressure when she'd demurred.

Even when darkness came, it had brought none of the problems she had frankly envisaged. In spite of his warning, Saul had been almost studious about avoiding any invasion of her privacy, in their shared part of the villa, although it had taken two anxious and sleepless nights before she'd realised that he had no immediate intention of persuading her to let him join her in that wide lovers' bed.

And thank heaven for Flawless cosmetics, she thought derisively, which had disguised the resulting shadows of restlessness beneath her eyes, and softened the line of strain along her cheekbones.

All the same, she was aware, as she'd been from the first, that he was only biding his time where she was concerned.

And now this was the last day of filming, she thought, touching her tongue delicately to the curve of her bottom lip. Tonight there would be a celebration at Yannis's taverna, and tomorrow she would be left here, alone with Saul.

Her stomach constricted nervously at the thought. Yet all her plans had been building inevitably, relentlessly, to just this moment. To having Saul at her mercy at last. To destroy his masculine pride, as surely as he'd ruined her vulnerable girlhood.

'Is something wrong?'

She had been so lost in her own thoughts that she hadn't heard his approach, and the quiet question made her start wildly.

'Wrong? No.' She found herself stammering. 'I— I'm fine. Everything's terrific.'

He studied her frowningly, his eyes missing nothing. 'Is it more of a strain that you expected, being the Flawless Girl?'

Carly shrugged. 'Perhaps. But nothing I can't handle. Although I'll be glad when this final shot is in the can.'

'So will I.' There was a note in his voice which made her pulses sharpen. A note of need, of anticipation. She stared down at the dusty ground, avoiding the intensity of his gaze. There was a silence, then Saul said more gently, 'Yet there's really nothing to worry about, darling. Sep Creed is delighted with you. So, just relax, and walk across the temple like the goddess you are.'

She attempted a little laugh. 'I don't feel much like a goddess. Besides—Aphrodite—wasn't she a blonde?'

'I wasn't thinking of Aphrodite,' Saul said. He took a small tissue-covered parcel from the pocket of his jeans and unwrapped it. 'This is for you. I saw it in the jeweller's shop in the village.'

A silver clasp shaped like a crescent moon lay in the palm of his hand.

Carly's lips parted in a small soundless gasp. 'It's—beautiful. But I can't take it.'

'Yes, you can.' Saul's voice was inexorable. 'It's to wear in your hair, like this.'

She had to struggle with herself not to recoil as he fastened the clasp into the gleaming mahogany strands.

'There you are.' His smile held a faint grimness as he surveyed her. 'Artemis personified.'

'Why Artemis?' The intimate brush of his fingers against her hair had produced its own devastating effect, she realised with dismay. Under the veiling of the white bodice, her breasts had tautened, the rosy peaks proud and all too visible beneath the thin material. A detail which, she saw, had not been lost on him.

'Because it seemed appropriate.' He paused, his eyes lingering almost ruefully on this unmistakable evidence of her arousal, then lifting to her flushing face. 'Artemis was a cool lady, too. One man who tried to get too close to her was torn to pieces for his trouble.'

Her mouth was suddenly dry. 'That sounds—incredibly violent.'

'They were violent days,' he said. 'Now we commit mayhem in a far more civilised manner, but the lasting effect is still the same.' His gaze held hers, challenging her suddenly.

He knows, she thought. But he can't, unless he's remembered that stupid trick with the glasses. And ever since then I've been so careful . . .

She said with a catch in her voice, 'And is that what you think I intend—mayhem?'

He said harshly, 'Lady, I'm damned if I know any more. You tell me.'

As he turned away, she heard the director call her name, and nerved herself, forcing the professional model to take over from the suddenly tremulous girl.

She moved across the uneven slabs of stone without faltering, using the smooth, half-floating walk she had learned so painstakingly, feeling the breeze tug effortlessly at her wispy draperies, making them cling ever closer to her slim body. She heard one of the crew whistle under his breath, and as she reached the tall pillar of stone, and placed her hand on it, she allowed herself to smile faintly, a woman secure in the conviction of her own beauty, her own sexuality.

There was a charged silence, then a brief spontaneous round of applause.

Jim, the director, said, 'I don't think we can better that, but we'll have to do another take as insurance, all the same.' He paused. 'Can you give it to us again, Carly, my love? That same combination of ice and sex?' He grinned at her. 'If it has the same effect on the viewing audience as it had on us, Flawless should sweep all the other cosmetic brands into oblivion.'

They were all so pleased with her, she realised with a heart-wrenching pang. So delighted with the way the project had gone. So excited with the campaign as a whole.

And, because of her, no one would ever see it. Oh, there would be a new campaign, and another Flawless Girl, but it wouldn't have the same quality, the same impact as this.

In fact, nothing would ever be the same again.

She thought, This will be the last time...

And, in that knowledge, Carly North retraced her steps, and gave the camera exactly what it wanted.

For their party that night, Yannis had barbecued a lamb, serving it with fresh crusty bread, still warm from the oven, and a variety of spicy, garlicky sauces. He'd strung coloured lights among the vine which twined across the taverna's roof, and placed candles in little glass holders on all the tables.

There was ouzo waiting for them, too, on the house.

'We drink,' Yannis beamed at them. 'To success, and to happiness—and that one day you all come back to Thyrsos.'

There was laughter and a muffled cheer as the toast was drunk. Carly only pretended to drink, keeping her fingers clamped for concealment round her glass. When no one was looking, she poured the ouzo away on the dusty floor beneath the table.

She couldn't drink that toast. She couldn't be such a hypocrite.

As she put the glass down, she saw Saul watching her, his brows drawn together. Had he seen what she'd done? she wondered feverishly. If so, it was time to divert his attention. Down the length of the table, she smiled at him, her face lighting up, her eyes sparking with mischief and frank seduction, and watched his expression relax, then change to a very different kind of tension.

Carly sent him one last provocative look under her lashes, then turned her attention to Septimus Creed's personal assistant, Julie, who was sitting next to her, openly bemoaning the fact that she was going home the next day.

'You're so lucky,' the other girl sighed. 'I bet it's raining non-stop in London.'

'I'm staying behind to work,' Carly reminded her, and Julie pulled a face.

'Some work,' she remarked naughtily. 'I wish providence had sent me a job like that. You wouldn't care to swap assignments?'

Yes, Carly thought savagely. Yes, I would. I'd give anything at this moment to have an ordinary job—to be happily engaged to a solicitor as you are, and be planning a summer wedding. To have no problem except finding a flat with enough room for your David's hi-fi and record collection.

She said quietly, 'A model's life isn't all it's cracked up to be. I've been lucky so far, but soon there'll be a dozen younger, prettier girls fighting their way past me.'

'And what will you do when that happens?'

Carly shrugged. 'My life's changed direction once. It can happen again.'

'You're not thinking in terms of marriage? You're so gorgeous, you must have loads of men after you.' Julie's tone was not flattering, merely stating the obvious.

Carly bent her head. 'Not as many as you'd think,' she said.

'Hm,' Julie said drily. 'Well, one obviously comes to mind, and not a million miles from this table, either.'

Colour stirred under Carly's skin. 'I don't know what you mean.'

Julie gave a soft hoot of laughter. 'Of course you do. He's absolutely obsessed by you—anyone can see that. I heard him saying to Jim that he felt he'd known you before—that he'd known you always.'

Carly's nails fastened painfully in the palms of her hands. Her throat tightened in alarm. She managed a laugh. 'Oh, dear. That sounds almost spooky.'

'Maybe,' Julie shrugged. 'But I thought it was really romantic.'

She turned to talk to someone else, leaving Carly alone with her thoughts.

They were far from comfortable.

When the meal was over, the tables were pushed back and there was dancing, led by Yannis and his sons. One by one the television crew were inveigled on to the floor, to receive a crash-course in the dipping, swaying movements and intricate footwork of the dance. Carly watched for a while, then slipped away out of the taverna on to the harbour wall, letting the music and laughter follow her.

The moon had risen, and was shining over the water in a rippling ribbon of silver.

Carly put up a hand and touched the crescent moon in her hair. She was wearing it loose this evening, letting it spill over her shoulders, with Saul's clasp keeping the heavy waves back from her forehead. Everyone had admired it, and she'd seen more than one smothered smile and significant glance being exchanged when she'd explained where it had come from.

Most of them, she realised, assumed that Saul and she were lovers already, and that the silver moon was some kind of intimate avowal—a token of long-term commitment. Whereas she knew it was just something else to be left behind in the ruins when the time came.

Pain slashed at her swiftly, and she drew a deep breath.

She thought, If Saul and I had met, in truth, for the first time that night at the Flawless reception— if there had been no burdens, no shadows from the past—it could all have been so different. It would have been so good—so right . . .

She stopped right there, her throat closing in shock and bewilderment bordering on panic, as she assimilated the tenor of her thoughts.

All this time she'd been telling herself that Saul had merely been the focus of her first tumultuous adolescent yearnings, and that was why his cruelty, his rejection of her had hurt so much—had damaged her so violently. That it was because of his treatment of her at that totally vulnerable time of her life that she'd found it impossible ever since to relate to any other man, however kind, caring or attentive he might be. Because Saul had smashed her dreams, and blighted the burgeoning impulses of her young sexuality.

He'd made her nothing, when she'd wanted to be everything to him.

But now the tables were turned, and suddenly she was in confusion.

She'd gone to meet him that night, hating him, deliberately using her face and body as the instruments of her revenge. What she hadn't allowed for was the residue of feeling lurking unacknowledged somewhere deep in her psyche. She hadn't bargained for the emotional charge that being with him would engender. She hadn't realised what would happen when he touched her—took her in his arms—kissed her. She hadn't known how he could make her feel.

She might look like a woman, but beneath the façade she was still the same vulnerable child she'd been when she first saw him—first loved him.

A groan of sheer anguish rose inside her, and was instantly stifled. What was she doing, allowing herself even to think like this? It was Julie's fault— talking all that sentimental nonsense about marriage.

Making her confront for the first time what might have been. The kind of happiness she could have had, if only...

No! The word was like a scream in her head. She hated Saul Kingsland, hated what he'd done to her. Her whole life had been based on that, dedicated to revenging herself on him.

Oh, dear heaven, surely she couldn't have been deceiving herself all this time? It just wasn't possible.

Oh, please, she prayed, as the moonlight on the water blurred, please don't let this be happening to me...

'Aren't you coming back to the party?'

Her whole body stiffened. She might have known that he would follow—seek her out. He was standing so close behind her, she knew, that all she'd have to do was turn and she would be in his arms.

She reached for a control she wasn't sure she possessed. 'I'm not really in a party mood.' *Heaven help me.* 'I hate the ending of things—goodbyes. I thought I might just slip away, back to the villa.'

'Shall I come with you?'

She shook her head. She was going to say, 'There's no need,' but the words stuck in her throat. Because there *was* a need in her, a necessity, an agony of yearning which filled the world.

And this man—this enemy whom she'd vowed to destroy in any way she could—was the only one who could satisfy that necessity, heal her and make her whole again.

Slowly, she turned to face him, taking one step backwards so that there was distance between them. Trying to make it safe. Failing.

She said, 'No—not now. Not tonight.'

'But soon.' He wasn't asking. He was telling her that the waiting was over.

She said his name on a little shaken sigh, and went from him, out of the moonlight to the darkness of the steep road back to the villa.

And, when she knew she was out of sight, she began to run.

Carly stood on the quayside, waving as Adonis manoeuvred his laughing, cheering boatload out towards the open sea. She had said goodbye, until she hated the sound of the word. She had smiled until her facial muscles ached with the strain.

And now it was over, and she was alone at the villa with Saul.

She swallowed thickly, aware that that deep inner trembling had begun all over again. It had plagued her throughout the previous night, keeping her from sleep, and this morning, she thought candidly, she looked a wreck.

Perhaps Saul thought so, too, because although he had made no overt comment, he had suggested they should take a day off, and spend it on the beach, relaxing.

It was a recommendation that fitted her own plans entirely.

The doubts that had assailed her last night had been deliberately relegated to some far corner of her mind. That had just been some inexplicable moment of weakness, she assured herself. And it meant nothing. All that mattered was achieving what she'd set out to do. That was what she had to remember. Not some nonsense about love and 'might have been'.

'They're a great crowd.' Smiling, Saul now came to stand beside her. 'It's good to think we'll be working with them again on the second stage of the campaign.'

Carly nodded, biting her lip.

'That, of course, is if there is a second stage,' he added, grinning.

'What do you mean?' She stared at him, eyes wide and startled.

He said ruefully, 'I meant if you survive the ride on the back of the bike down to that beach I mentioned to you. It was intended as a joke, but it was obviously a bad one.' He put a hand lightly on her shoulder. 'Loosen up, darling. Thyrsos was meant to be a relaxing experience for you, but most of the time you're so tensed up I'm afraid you'll snap.'

She shrugged slightly, moving away, releasing herself. 'I've never been the pivot of a campaign before. Maybe I am feeling the pressure, as you said.'

'Well, now the pressure's off—in every way,' he said quietly. 'I couldn't sleep last night for thinking about you—your face as you left me. You looked— stricken, as if I'd pronounced sentence of death. Darling, you know I want you, but it has to be mutual. Haven't I made that clear?'

Her heart skipped a beat. He was letting her off the hook again, and playing right into her hands.

She bent her head. 'Of course you have. I'm such an idiot.'

'No.' His voice was gentle. 'You're just much younger than you look, my sweet, and heartbreakingly innocent. Lord knows how you've preserved that in the rat race we both belong to, but I hope it's something you never lose, or not emotionally, at least,' he added, his mouth twisting wryly.

Carly bent swiftly to retrieve her beach-bag in order to conceal her rising blush. 'Well—shall we be going?'

Her hair streamed behind her as she rode on the pillion behind him to the beach. The bumpy road with its pot-holes, little better than a track, was hardly the ideal introduction to motorbike riding, she decided breathlessly, but the beach itself was idyllic, and well worth the jolting.

It was probably the only stretch of pure sand anywhere round the island, and totally deserted. Saul left the bike in a grove of olive trees, and they walked together down the path, bordered by scrub which led to the beach.

She said teasingly, 'I see you've brought your cameras. I thought today was going to be a holiday.'

He grimaced. 'They're like an extension of myself. I never seem able to abandon them entirely. Do you mind?'

'Not a bit.' Today, after all, it was no more than the truth.

Carly spread out her towel, then began to unbutton the black thigh-length muslin shirt she was wearing. She took her time, aware that Saul, already stripped down to brief trunks, was watching every movement. Underneath the shirt she was wearing a bikini, also in black. She had searched London until she'd found exactly what she wanted.

It was the least she'd ever worn in her life, the bra top so minimal that it barely contained the thrust of her firm breasts, and the briefs consisting of two skimpy triangles which tied with strings on her slender hips.

There was incredulity as well as hunger in Saul's eyes as he studied her, and her body warmed involuntarily under the frankness of his scrutiny.

'Do you approve?' She smiled with enforced gaiety, trying to hide her sudden self-consciousness.

He said slowly, 'I think approval is hardly the right word. I'm—overwhelmed.'

'I think you're exaggerating. You must have seen and photographed hundreds of girls wearing this amount—or less.'

'If so, I don't remember.'

Think back, she adjured him silently. Think back a few summers to a country wedding, and a girl called Katie, who stripped for you in the sunlight before you—you . . .

At the thought, as always, she felt the lash of the old familiar pain, the surge of nausea she had no defence against. Her hands clenched harshly into fists as she fought for control, and won.

She laughed. 'I don't think I'll be very flattered if you forget me as easily.'

'You,' Saul said, 'I can never forget. You're etched on my consciousness for all eternity, and beyond.'

There was a note in his voice which sent an almost feverish ripple of excitement shivering through her body. She crushed it down.

'Wouldn't a photograph be a simpler way of keeping the memory intact?' She sent him a demure look under her lashes.

He grimaced, half-wryly, half-humorously. 'At this moment, my sweet, I doubt if I could hold the camera steady. I think I'll go for a swim, and cool off a little.'

Carly watched him walk down the narrow strip of beach to the edge of the water.

There's no hurry, she reminded herself. There's plenty of time. Take it easy.

She put some more sunblock on her arms and legs, then lay down on her towel, face downwards. To her surprise, she found her thoughts beginning to drift. The peace of the place must be getting to her, she thought drowsily, or maybe it was just her disturbed night catching up with her. Whatever it was, closing her eyes for a few minutes couldn't do any harm. No harm at all.

She woke some time later to a familiar sound— the click and whirr of a camera's shutter. Saul was sitting a few yards away, his face intent as he focused on her.

She sat up with a gasp. 'What on earth are you doing?'

'Photographing Sleeping Beauty,' he said promptly. 'I'm sure the Prince would have done so, if cameras had been invented then.'

'Well, for her sake, I'm glad they weren't. I think you've taken an unfair advantage.' She pouted at him. 'I bet I had my mouth open, and was snoring.'

He said slowly, 'You looked like a little girl again.'

Something clenched in the pit of her stomach. 'You don't know that. You've no idea what I looked like when I was a little girl.'

'People don't change that much, surely,' he said. 'I could make an educated guess.'

Carly looked at him, held his gaze, smiled at him, moistening her lips with the tip of her tongue. 'But I'm really not a child—not any more.' She ran her hands lightly over her body. 'Look.'

'I'm looking.' His voice was suddenly grim.

'You don't seem totally convinced.' Her heart was hammering. She was excited and frightened in equal proportions at the prospect of what she was about to do. 'Maybe I should offer you proof that I'm a woman.'

She reached up, undid the clasp of her bikini top as she'd seen Katie do that day, and let the scrap of material drop to the sand beside her, every movement a deliberate imitation of the scene which had seared itself into her consciousness like an open wound. She was playing with fire. Surely—now— he must remember? Or was Katie just one in a line of nubile girls taken cynically, and discarded without a second thought? The possibility sent anger mingled with anguish scorching through her body.

Oh, she would make him pay, not just for himself, but for all men who thought they could use women lightly, then walk away.

She damped down the flare of rage inside her, and stretched, lithely, provocatively. She said softly, 'Is that better?'

'Exquisite.' His tone was raw.

'Then why not make the most of me?' Her voice deliberately teased him. 'Wouldn't you like your own personal and private portfolio of the Flawless Girl?'

'I wouldn't express it in quite those terms.'

'Then how?'

He said slowly, 'The beginning, perhaps, of a lifetime's study.'

Her mouth was bone-dry, the muscles in her throat tautening painfully. This wasn't the reaction she'd expected. That wasn't what she'd wanted to hear. She said with an effort, 'That sounds—serious.'

'It was intended to.'

She tried to laugh, to lighten the moment, but no sound would come. Suddenly there was silence, enclosing them, cocooning them. An intense, deafening silence, containing nothing but the beat of her heart and his.

His gaze held hers, sending a message of stark yearning, of almost helpless need.

Carly felt as if invisible cords had tightened round her, drawing her to him, her mouth on his, her hands on his body. She seemed weightless, suddenly, boneless, as if her entire physicality had been poured, concentrated, into some central core of sensation which was crying out for appeasement.

She was drowning in honey, entangled in some warm, sweet, golden web, caught in the spell of her own devising.

And that could not be.

She dredged up some forgotten reserve of willpower, and moved, curving her body with deliberate seduction, forcing herself back into control.

She said, and was amazed to hear how normal her voice sounded, 'You're keeping me waiting, Mr Kingsland.'

He said quietly, menacingly, 'Am I?' and picked up his camera.

She had never experienced anything like it before. Within seconds, she knew that somehow, yet again, she'd lost the whip hand, and that Saul was back in command. He was totally merciless, making her give as she'd never done before, his voice sometimes husky, often harsh as he encouraged and demanded. Before the session was half over, Carly felt emotionally limp, the sweat pouring from her body, but there was no rest, no respite. She had offered herself as an object to be photographed, and as such he took her.

'Had enough?' he flung at her at last.

'Have you?' She wiped the perspiration from her eyes.

'It would take eternity for that.' There was no humour in his smile. 'But I think we've exhausted the possibilities of this session.'

'Not quite.' She knelt upright, composing herself, letting the flurry of her breathing steady, resting her hands on her waist. She said, 'You'd better reload the camera,' and allowed her fingers to slide with slow deliberation down to her hips, where the little black bows waited to be untied. 'Won't you— help me?'

'No.' The denial came from him with such force, such a surge of uncontrollable emotion, that Carly's head snapped back as if he'd hit her. Her fingers stilled.

She said, stammering a little, 'What's the matter. What's wrong?'

His voice was molten. 'You dare ask me that?'

'You've photographed nude women before.' There had been an exhibition of his work in conjunction with some other contemporary photographers at a London gallery. Saul Kingsland's nudes and the erotic charge they conveyed had been one of the talking points. She'd looked at them, and remembered, and used those memories to fuel her bitterness, her vengefulness.

'That was different.'

'How?' she hurled back in challenge.

'We are not,' he said, too softly, 'talking about an exercise in aesthetics. The first time, lady, that I see you naked, it will not be through the lens of my camera. That I swear.'

There was a brief, electric pause, then he added, in a tone that permitted no argument. 'Now get your clothes on. We're going back.'

Her fingers shook as she fastened her bikini top, and slid into her shirt. Out of the corner of her eye, she watched Saul stow the used rolls of film away in his canvas bag. Noted carefully and exactly where he put them. Took a little shuddering breath.

She hadn't achieved the whole of what she'd set out to do, but it was enough, surely, to bring the Flawless campaign crashing down, and Saul's career with it when those pictures of her appeared as the next Sunday Siren in Mark Clayfield's *Globe*.

I've won, she thought. And found herself wondering why, at the very moment of triumph, she should feel such an odd sense of defeat.

CHAPTER NINE

THE villa was very quiet. Carly sat on the edge of her bed, listening to the silence with growing unease.

It had been a strange, solitary afternoon. She'd spent most of it by the pool. But Saul had not joined her there. According to Penelope, who had appeared at intervals with iced drinks, Kyrios Saul had gone off once more on his motorcycle. It was clear she disapproved of such intense activity in the full heat of the day. It was also obvious that she regarded Saul's defection as thoroughly unloverlike behaviour. Although Penelope had more reason than most people to know that she and Saul were not, in fact, lovers at all, Carly thought, biting her lip.

But at least Saul's absence had meant that she'd had a chance to speak privately to Adonis on his return, and arrange for him to take her in his boat to Mykonos at first light the following day. She'd invented a story about arranging a surprise for Kyrios Saul—'A special surprise, Adonis'—and had little trouble in enlisting his support.

And by the time Adonis received the message she planned to leave for him at the harbour—that she had decided to spend a day or two on Mykonos—and returned to Thyrsos without her, it would be too late for Saul to come after her. And, even when he did follow, he wouldn't find her, she thought, her nerves tightening.

Because by then she would be safely back in London, and Mark Clayfield would have those sexy, damaging rolls of film, fully attributable to Saul Kingsland, to use just as he wanted.

And after that . . .

Her mind closed off. She didn't want to contemplate what would happen after that. It frightened her to realise what she'd set in motion. Some kind of serious legal action was only one possibility. Whatever the outcome, even if Saul proved that he hadn't given permission for the pictures to be used, his professional integrity would still be severely damaged.

Among those who would also inevitably suffer in the aftermath were Clive and Marge, and the realisation of that tore at her. They were the last people she wanted to hurt.

And her family too would writhe in the glare of the unavoidable publicity, once those pictures appeared, she thought drily. So it would be no use seeking sanctuary from Saul's anger at their home. She would not be welcome there. Might never be welcome again.

So many boats to burn in this, her personal holocaust.

But it will be worth it, she told herself, in a kind of panic. It has to be worth it. Doesn't it?

She waited for the inner reassurance that never failed; for the small, stony voice which told her that the end justified the means, no matter what other harm might be done. The voice that said Saul Kingsland deserved everything that was coming to him, and more.

But this time there was only that brooding silence.

Carly shivered, folding her arms defensively across her body. For the first time she found herself facing the fact that the person who might be most seriously damaged by what she was planning was herself.

Flawless would undoubtedly sue her for breach of contract, but she was prepared for that. What she couldn't predict was what psychological scars her quest for revenge on Saul might leave on her. She had only looked forward to the moment when he realised she had betrayed him totally, as he'd once betrayed her. Never beyond.

She had never considered the fact that, when it was all over, she would have to live with herself. Not merely build some kind of new life, but come to terms with what she'd done.

Why am I thinking like this now? she asked herself wildly. Why this moment—when I've achieved what I set out to do?

Not quite, she reminded herself. She still had to retrieve the rolls of film from Saul's bag. But that wouldn't present any great difficulty.

She glanced at her watch. Only a few more hours, she thought, swallowing. Only a few. No wonder I'm so tense.

She got up, and went towards the window. On the small dressing-chest, something glinted, cool and silver. Carly picked up the moon clasp, holding the crescent in the palm of her hand, staring down at it. Then, obeying an impulse she barely understood, she fastened it into her hair.

Penelope had set a table on the terrace overlooking the sea. Carly perched on the wall, and stared towards the horizon. Thyrsos was really

Paradise in miniature, she thought. If only things had been different, she could have been so happy here. With Saul.

She tried to block the words out, to deny them, but it was impossible. Whether she wanted to or not, she had to face the fact that Saul Kingsland was the only man in the world she had ever wanted, or ever would want. The bitter irony of it screamed at her.

How many times had it been said that there was only a thin dividing line between love and hate? It had become a cliché, but it also contained a terrible truth.

She had loved Saul, and then she had hated him with a kind of devouring madness. And now the two emotions were so inextricably confused in her mind that she didn't know what to think—what to feel.

The night was warm, but she felt cold, chilled to the bone, and she was trembling inside again, a prey to sensations she could neither explain or rationalise away. Saul was her enemy—the man who'd betrayed her—driven her to the extreme of changing her life completely. That was simple. That was what had motivated her all this time. So how was it possible that she could want him—need him, this enemy of hers—with such devastating completeness?

Penelope brought her retsina in a little copper pot, and she poured some into a glass and sipped it gratefully. She'd grown to like the strong resinated flavour of the wine. She wanted the warmth it engendered to drive the cold and the trembling away. But tonight, it seemed, it was not the panacea she needed.

'I'm sorry if I've kept you waiting for dinner.' Saul's voice was as formal as the words as he came to join her. He was wearing close-fitting cream trousers and a black shirt, left casually unbuttoned at the throat. His hair was damp, and Carly was aware of the sharp fragrance of soap and cologne commingled with the warm, intensely personal scent of his skin.

Her mouth went dry. It was so long—too long—since she'd been in his arms, she thought crazily. She wanted to be close to him, held by him, her face buried in the hollow between his neck and shoulder, breathing him, absorbing him through every pore.

And she couldn't—couldn't...

'Did you have a pleasant afternoon?' he went on, after a pause.

'Restful.' They were talking like polite strangers.

'I'm glad.' Another silence. Then he said, quietly, 'I'm sorry I allowed everything to get so fraught this morning. From the first moment I saw you, I wanted you. But you know that already. What I've never told you before is that it was like a homecoming—as if I'd found the other half of myself. But I kept telling myself that it would be all right—that I could work with you, and remain impersonal and professional about it all.' He laughed in self-derision. 'Well, now you know I can't. That's why I cleared out this afternoon. I knew I couldn't be with you—spend any more time with you, and not—touch you.' His voice was uneven suddenly.

'More than touch. So I rode around the island on the bike, and did some serious thinking.'

A shaky smile touched the corners of her mouth. 'No photography?'

'I didn't even take the cameras,' he said wryly. 'I couldn't see anything but you, anyway. You're inside my head, under my skin.' His hand lifted, and the long fingers touched the curve of her jaw, slowly, tentatively. He whispered, 'What are you doing to me? What are we doing to each other?'

She said his name, half under her breath, feeling it torn out of the ache in her chest, of the pain deep within her.

She saw some of the strain, some of the rigidity leave his face. Saw his mouth curve with a new gentleness as he bent towards her.

Then the shadows of the terrace were invaded, put to flight by light from within the villa, and Penelope was bustling out with a tray holding two steaming soup bowls.

'*Avgholemono,*' she announced, beaming, waving a hand at the pale, creamy liquid. 'You both eat good.'

Saul grinned at Carly, his expression both humorous and rueful. His mouth shaped the word, 'Later.'

The meal seemed endless, although they did not attempt to hurry it in any way. A covenant between them had been made, and would be kept. Carly knew that now, knew that it had always been inevitable, and with acceptance came a kind of peace. There would be no regrets, no wondering to pursue her into her new life. She would possess, and be possessed, and after that she would be free.

In the meantime, there was a strange, tantalising pleasure in facing him across the small lamplit table, and enjoying the food with him. And tonight Penelope had surpassed herself. The soup with its rich lemony flavour was succeeded by vine leaves stuffed with rice and meat, and then fish, baked in the oven. For dessert there was fruit, luscious peaches nestling among dark green leaves, and purple grapes, large as plums and sweet as honey. They drank white wine, dry and cool, which lingered on the palate, and ended the meal with tiny cups of thick Greek coffee, and a liqueur, redolent of tangerines.

As Carly drained her cup, she was aware of a tingling anticipation, half-pleasurable, half-fearful. Like the sensation, she thought, when the car of a rollercoaster reaches the crest, just before that wild plunge downwards into the unknown.

Saul pushed back his chair, and came round the table to her. He took her hand and pulled her gently to her feet, his eyes searching hers for any sign of withdrawal. With his other hand, he unpinned the crescent moon from her hair, and left it on the table. He said quietly, 'No virgin goddess tonight.'

He led her from the terrace to the steep, vine-shadowed steps, and up to the balcony above. The air was very still and warm. She could hear the rasping of the cicadas in the garden and, looking up, saw the full moon rising over the sea, like a serene face bestowing a pagan blessing. She thought, I'll remember this always...

She had half expected Saul to stop at the open window of her room, but he didn't even pause there.

Instead he took her to the end of the balcony, and his own room, where she had never been.

There was a lamp lit beside the bed, bathing the starkness of the snowy sheet and pillows with a soft radiance.

Her heart thudded in sudden alarm. Like a set for a play, she thought stupidly, staring at the bed. Only I don't know any of my lines. I don't know what to do. I don't know...

She didn't realise she'd said the last words aloud, until Saul said gently, 'We'll learn together, darling. Trust me.'

He kissed her softly at first, barely moving his mouth on hers. But soon, so soon, it was not enough. Carly wound her arms round his neck, pressing herself against him, feeling her soft breasts bloom to aching life against the hard wall of his chest.

She felt the stroke of his tongue along her lips, coaxing them to part for him, and she obeyed as a sweet delirium invaded her veins, turning her blood to fire.

They clung together, mouths and tongues searching and demanding almost frantically. She felt Saul's hands begin a slow, intimate pilgrimage down the length of her body. He touched her briefly, caressingly through her dress, his fingers lingering on her breasts, adoring the surge of her hardening nipples against the friction of the thin fabric, forcing a small, harsh sound of pleasure from her throat.

His hands moved down, as if memorising the planes and contours of ribcage, waist and stomach, and she swayed in his arms, oblivious to everything but the passage of those lingering, tormenting fingers. He traced the outline of her hips and the gentle swell of her buttocks, and a new, moist heat flared inside her. She moved against him in silent pleading, experiencing the stark urgency of his arousal through the minimal layers of clothing which separated them, but that was no appeasement for the hunger that tore at her. Her need was as fierce as his own.

His hand parted her thighs and found the cleft of her womanhood, and she cried out, her body convulsing in a pleasure she'd never before known, or even imagined.

He whispered her name against her mouth, then lifted her and carried her to the bed. He lay beside her, cupping her face in both hands, kissing her with a hot and hungry urgency. Carly held him, her slender body straining against his, her fingers gripping his shoulders. Her eyes were tightly closed, and little golden lights danced behind her lids.

When he lifted his head, she looked up at him dazedly. Saul smiled into her eyes, then slid one hand down to her waist to find the sash that fastened her simple wraparound dress, and tug it free.

The dress fell open, and he drew a sharp, uneven breath as he looked at her. He let his hand venture slowly, almost teasingly, down the valley between her breasts, then began to brush the creamy swell very gently with his fingertips. It was the simplest of caresses, but her whole body responded fiercely and wantonly to his touch.

His eyes fixed on her face, Saul began to trace a finger round each swollen dusky aureole in turn, his touch delicate and very exact. Never, even accidentally, did he allow his hand to stray to the aroused and aching peak. Yet she wanted him there—oh, so badly. She tried to speak, to tell him so, and he bent and silenced her with his mouth, before continuing his sweet, erotic torment.

She pushed her hands inside his shirt, feeling a button tear, but not caring as she slid her palms across the hair-roughened skin of his chest, then up to the broad, muscled sweep of his shoulders.

He felt so good, she thought, the breath catching in her throat. So strong, and utterly male. And she'd been waiting so long for this moment—all the days of her life . . .

He kissed her again, without haste, flicking his tongue sensuously across her parted lips, then bent his head, kissing each soft, scented mound before taking one proud, rosy nipple into his mouth.

She made a small, inarticulate sound as she felt the stroke of his tongue against her tumescent flesh, exciting, inciting sensations she had not known existed until this moment. She cradled his dark head in her hands, holding him to her breasts, her body arching in painful delight as he sucked more deeply, and she felt the faint graze of his teeth against her skin.

She thought crazily, I can't bear this. I can't . . . But if he stops, I'll die.

He slipped an arm underneath her, lifting her slightly so that he could free her completely from the hampering folds of her dress. He let it drop to the floor beside the bed, then sent his shirt to join it. He knelt over her, spreading her arms wide so that he could trace, with his lips, the whole of their slender length. She felt his tongue exploring her palms, the pulses going crazy at her wrists, the bend of her elbow, the hollow of her armpit, and the curve of her neck and shoulder.

She began to touch his back, running her hands over her shoulderblades, then down the curve of his spine, and he whispered his pleasure into the whorls of her ear, biting at its lobe.

He kissed her mouth, then caressed her breasts softly with his lips as his hands stroked down her body.

Deftly, gently, he removed her last flimsy covering, and for a moment shyness overwhelmed her as he looked at her, and she tried to turn her head away.

His fingers reached out instantly, capturing her chin, making her face the burning intensity in his eyes.

'No.' His voice sounded raw, suddenly. 'You can't hide from me now, my darling. It's too late. You're too beautiful.'

Tenderly, his hand found the warm moistness of her, and began a new and devastating exploration.

All the breath seemed to leave her body. Awareness receded to some far, dangerous distance. Nothing existed for her, except the silken, tantalising stroke of Saul's fingers. She was no longer in control, she recognised as she began to move wantonly and crazily against his caressing hand. She didn't even belong to herself any more. She was his creation, half-toy, half-animal. An instrument of pleasure of his designing, and made for him, only him.

There was a dark, savage ache—an overwhelming need—building, spiralling inside her. Every sense in her being seemed to be channelled suddenly and sharply—driven inexorably towards the fulfilment of that need.

Then she was there, at the edge of the unknown, and for a moment she was afraid. The spiral rose inside her in a final crescendo that was half-agony, and half-delight. She found herself taken, consumed by it, wrenched apart, and then released, as her body was racked by convulsion after convulsion of quivering, burning pleasure.

She lay dazed and drained, listening to the hammer of her own pulse-beats, hardly able to believe the maelstrom of sensation which had possessed and almost destroyed her. Reality returned slowly, languidly.

And reality was Saul lying next to her, naked himself now as any pagan god. He gathered her to him, and his mouth claimed hers, deeply and passionately. She clung to him, kissing him back without inhibition. She felt the heat and power of his maleness pressing against her pliant thighs, and realised, almost with shock, that what she had experienced was only a beginning. Suddenly, and starkly, she wanted him inside her. Had to have him there.

She touched him in wonderment, shaping the power of him with her fingers, and his hand covered hers, halting her.

He said huskily, 'Darling, I can wait.'

'Why?' Acting on pure instinct, she lifted her legs to enfold him. Saul gasped, and heated colour flared along his cheekbones. He said her name on a shaken breath, and entered her with one deep, fluid thrust.

There was no pain. Just a sense of total completeness, and for a while they remained still in each other's arms, mouths gently brushing, bodies locked together in the final intimacy.

When Saul did begin to move, it was slowly at first, tempering his needs to her inexperience.

Her body felt like some fathomless cavern of the ocean, and he was the strong tide which ebbed and flowed within it. The kisses they exchanged were warm and languorous. Saul's hands cupped her breasts, fondling the nipples into vibrant, aching life, making her moan softly.

The sound of her voice, hoarse with desire, seemed to tip him over some brink. He was holding back no longer, his body plundering hers with harsh and fevered hunger, and she surrendered eagerly to the delicious, brutal rhythm of his possession, echoing each heated thrust, arms and legs gripping him fiercely.

This was for him, she found herself thinking. Solely and wholly for him.

But even as the thought took shape in her mind, it was already too late. The first, intense spasms of delight were overtaking her once more, tearing her slowly into a thousand, minute, shimmering pieces and flinging her out into some blinding golden cosmos where the last thing she was aware of was Saul's own triumphant cry of fulfilment.

This time, the descent from the heights took longer. She found there were tears on her face as she lay in his arms, and he kissed them away.

'Did I hurt you?' he whispered. 'Darling, did I hurt you?'

'No.' Sated, relaxed and more at peace with herself than she could ever remember, she lifted a hand and stroked the line of his jaw. 'Oh, no. I'm just—so happy, that's all.' She paused, shy again. 'Saul—I—I never knew—never thought it could be like that.'

'Then that makes two of us.' He cuddled her closer.

'But that can't be right,' she said slowly. 'You've had so many women...'

He propped himself up on one elbow, and stared down at her, visibly startled.

'What gives you that idea? I'm far from being a virgin, it's true, but reports of my conquests have been greatly exaggerated. I've had a few fairly serious relationships, but I've never gone in for casual sex, or one-night stands.'

She wanted to cry out, And what about Katie? Does your encounter with her qualify as a serious relationship? The cocoon of joy and peace enclosing her was shattered. She was remembering, if she had ever forgotten, what she had to do.

She said, 'I suppose these days, it just isn't safe.'

'There's that aspect,' he agreed levelly. 'But I'd already decided how I intended to live my personal life, long before the AIDS scare.' He paused. 'And while we're speaking with such frankness, may I ask if you, my darling, are on the Pill?'

'Of course not,' she denied indignantly. 'I've never needed to be...' Her voice trailed away. 'Oh.'

'Oh, indeed,' Saul mocked, running a lazy hand over her flat stomach. 'I wonder, now...'

'It couldn't possibly have happened,' she said, half to herself.

'Couldn't it?' He dropped a kiss on her hair. 'I rather go for the idea myself. Don't you?'

'No.' The sound was like a yelp of anguish, and Saul's brows lifted.

He said very evenly, 'I love you, Carly, and I want to marry you. If you don't need that kind of commitment, what are you doing in my bed?'

Exorcising a personal demon, she could have answered. Instead, she remained silent, gnawing at her lower lip.

At last, she said feebly, 'I—couldn't fulfil the Flawless contract if I was pregnant.'

'I've seen some radiant pregnant women. Photographed them, too.' He paused. 'But if you feel strongly about it, then we'll take precautions from now on. Your contract doesn't have a clause forbidding marriage.' He tilted her chin up, making her look at him. 'Well?'

'It's too soon.' Her lips felt dry, and she moistened them with the tip of her tongue. 'You don't really know me...'

He gave her a faint grin. 'I was under the impression that I'd just known you as intimately as it's possible to do and still go on living.'

'I didn't mean that,' she said desperately. 'You don't know the kind of person I am—my background—all that kind of thing.'

'I know you have a pretty weird family, who don't seem to give a damn about you,' he said bluntly. 'I also know you've been hurt in the not-so distant past.' He stroked an errant tress of hair back from her forehead. 'I intend to make up for the one, and heal the other.' He stretched. 'Think about it while I take a shower. Unless, of course, you want to join me.'

She shook her head. 'It might be better if I—I went back to my own room now.'

'I'd rather you stayed here.' His mouth twisted wryly. 'Under the circumstances, I won't make love to you again, but I'd like to hold you while we sleep.'

Her heart skipped a wild beat. 'Saul—please, I'm so confused. I need some time on my own to think—to decide.'

'Have it, then,' he said, letting her go with obvious reluctance. He smiled at her. 'Just as long as you reach the right decision in the end.'

He got out of bed, lithe and naked. A beautiful, graceful animal, Carly thought, as unlooked-for hunger awoke within her again, and in the hunter's sights . . .

She said, 'Saul, those pictures you took this morning—you won't get them muddled with the other films, will you?'

He stopped at the bathroom door, and stared back at her. 'No, of course not. They're just between the two of us.'

'I couldn't bear anyone else to see them.' She knew she was gabbling. 'Couldn't I have them—look after them, just in case?'

He went on watching her, a slight frown twisting his brows, then he shrugged. 'If it'll make you happy, help yourself.'

She waited until she heard the water running, then she left the bed, pulling on her dress, and tying the sash anyhow.

She took the small canisters out of his bag, and looked down at them. In the end, how simple it had been. She'd only had to ask.

'If it'll make you happy.' The words seemed to reverberate in her brain.

And later, as she lay alone and sleepless in the darkness, waiting for dawn and the arrival of Adonis with his boat, she knew, sadly, and finally, that with Saul she'd been given her only chance of happiness. And that now she had lost it forever.

CHAPTER TEN

THE offices of the *Sunday Globe* were housed in an anonymous glass and concrete building near the docks.

Mark Clayfield was on the telephone when she arrived, and Caroline had to wait in his secretary's office.

'Couldn't I just leave the films with you?' she asked, wishing that she'd sent them over by messenger. 'I'm in rather a hurry.'

'I'm sure Mr Clayfield will want to speak to you.' The woman gave her an impersonal smile. She was neatly dressed, and rather staid-looking—the last person in the world Caroline could imagine working for a rag like the *Globe*.

But then, who am I to talk? she thought, feeling faintly sick.

Her departure from Thyrsos and the flight back to the UK had gone like clockwork. All the Fates seemed to be conspiring with her. And although she was tired from the flight, and wanted a bath and a change of clothes, she'd decided to make a detour on her way from the airport, and drop off the films to Mark Clayfield.

She wanted to be rid of them, she told herself defensively. Once she'd handed them over, that was the end of it. Her life as Carly North was finished, and she was free to begin again. And that was all there was to it. There was no question of being tempted to change her mind, which was the case the longer the films remained in her possession, and renege on her bargain with the *Globe*.

She glanced at her watch, wondering what time it was in Greece, and whether realisation had yet dawned on Saul that she was not coming back. She bit her lip. She could only count on a few more hours' leeway. Somehow she had to vanish, and as yet she had little idea where or how.

The buzzer sounded on the secretary's desk, and she rose. 'Will you go in now, please?'

Mark Clayfield was standing in front of a VDU screen as Caroline entered. He turned, the pale eyes flicking down her body, missing nothing.

'The films, as promised,' she said, putting them down on his desk.

'I can't wait to see them.' He smiled at her. 'Are they nude or just topless?'

'You said topless would be sufficient,' she reminded him evenly.

'So I did,' he said. 'But a man can dream, can't he?' He paused. 'Profitable session, was it? Did you and the dashing Mr Kingsland—get on all right?'

'You asked for photographs,' Caroline said curtly. 'Salacious details I'm sure you can invent for yourself, as usual.'

He laughed. 'We're on the same side, sweetie, remember?' He gave her a speculative look. 'I don't doubt Mr Kingsland's talent, but his work generally errs on the side of good taste. I hope these pictures will be raunchy enough for our readers.'

'Can they actually read?' Caroline felt suddenly as if she'd been dipped in slime. 'I thought they were merely voyeurs.'

'Heavens, we are sharp today.' He put the films in his desk drawer. 'What I was going to say was—if we require some—additional material to spice up the spread a little, where can we contact you?'

'You can't,' she said icily. 'What you see is what you get. Goodbye, Mr Clayfield.'

'I hope it's *au revoir*,' he called after her as she walked to the door. 'If we get a good response to you on Sunday, I'm sure we'll want to use you again—persuade you to bare all for us next time.'

Suddenly her stomach was heaving, and there was a hot, acrid taste in her mouth. She managed to say to the secretary, 'Is there a ladies' room somewhere?' and just made it to the toilet cubicle before she was violently sick.

'Are you all right? Would you like a glass of water, or some coffee, perhaps?' The secretary was hovering, clearly anxious, when she emerged.

Caroline gave her a pallid smile. 'I think the flight must have upset me,' she said mendaciously. 'I'd just like to go home, if someone could call me a cab.'

The flat was empty when she got in. Caroline walked into the sitting-room and looked round. There were flowers on the table by the window, and a certain amount of cheerful clutter, which meant that Lucy was back from abroad.

Caroline was thankful that her flatmate was out, probably at the television studios. She didn't want to have to talk to anyone—to pretend, or offer explanations.

She took her travel bag into the bedroom, and emptied it more or less piecemeal into the linen basket. She would cope with that at some future time, she thought, as she went into the bathroom and began to run water into the tub.

It was like some ritual cleansing ceremony. Caroline scrubbed herself from head to foot, until her skin was pink and glowing. She even shampooed her hair, digging her fingers into her scalp.

As she dried herself, she caught sight of herself in the mirror. Saw the taut lines of her mouth, and the shadows under her eyes.

Is it enough? she thought. Will I ever be really clean again?

Somehow, she doubted it.

She felt tears stinging at the back of her eyes, and rigorously dammed them back. It was too late to worry about that now. All her bridges were burned. There was no way back. Perhaps there never had been.

She should be rejoicing, she told herself, as she put on fresh underwear, and tied back her still-damp hair with a black ribbon bow at the nape of her neck. She should be in a champagne mood, not feeling deathly cold and sick like this—and somehow—desperate.

Perhaps this is how you feel when you've murdered someone, she thought, as she dragged on jeans, and fastened a white cotton shirt. This terrible feeling of hopelessness.

Because in a way, I am a murderess. I've killed Saul's love for me. It's the only thing I've ever been offered that I wanted, and I've strangled it at birth—thrown it away.

Her whole body clenched in grief and longing as she remembered her last glimpse of him.

It had been stupid and dangerous, because he might have woken and seen her, but she hadn't been able to resist the temptation to go back to his room to say a silent goodbye.

He'd been asleep, lying on his side, face and body relaxed and defenceless, one arm thrown across the space in the bed beside him. As if he was seeking her, she'd thought with a pang. And he was smiling slightly as he slept. It had taken every atom of will-power she possessed not to reach down and kiss that smile.

Her whole being, mind, body and spirit, seemed to be crying out to him, urging him to wake and prevent her from ruining both their lives.

Instead she had stood in the window, with slow, scalding tears running down her face, trying to re-member why she'd hated him—why revenge had seemed so overwhelmingly, so all-consumingly im-portant. She'd watched him until she could bear no more. Then she'd gone, like the thief in the night that she was.

She found her weekend case, and packed it economically and methodically with the minimum she would need for her few days in hiding. When the *Globe* came out on Sunday with her pictures, there would be no point in remaining in seclusion any longer. She would have to face the music.

All she could hope was that Saul would be so angry—so bitter—that he would never want to see her again. She couldn't bear to face him, to see the condemnation in his eyes.

She tied a sweater across her shoulders. The skies over London were grey, and after Thyrsos the wind had an edge to it. She picked up her case, then paused. There were two last things she still had to do before she was free to run.

She wrote a brief note to Lucy, explaining she'd gone away for a little while, but would be in touch, and left it propped on the kitchen table.

Then she took the photograph of herself as a young girl out of its frame, and took one final, steady look at the gauche, vulnerable face. She tore it across, then tore it again, and dropped the fragments into her waste-basket.

'The end,' she said aloud. 'That's the end.'

She took her case, and carried it down to the car.

The inn's car park was nearly full when she arrived. Caroline slotted the Polo neatly between a Porsche and a Range Rover, and sat for a moment, looking around her.

She still wasn't sure why she'd come here. She'd found herself driving on autopilot most of the way. It seemed almost Freudian to have chosen this, of all villages, but the inn would do as a refuge for the night at least. She doubted whether she was capable of driving on further.

She got out and retrieved her bag, then, hunching her shoulders against the persistent drizzle which had followed her from London, she sprinted for the door marked 'Accommodation'.

She found herself in a carpeted passage with a neat reception desk facing her at its end. She rang the bell, and a girl in a dark skirt and white blouse appeared, and smiled at her.

'Can I help you?'

'I'd like a room. I suppose I should have phoned, really...'

'Oh, we're rarely that full midweek, and it's still early in the season.' The girl found a registration card and handed it to Caroline with a pen. 'How long were you wanting to stay?'

Caroline shrugged. 'My plans are fairly fluid. Could we just play it by ear?'

'Whatever suits you.' The girl paused. 'They're all double rooms, but we'd only charge for single occupation.' Briskly she ran through the tariff, and got Caroline to show her credit card. 'We've got quite a crowd in for dinner tonight, but if you wanted to eat, we could probably squeeze you in about nine-thirty.'

Caroline shook her head. 'I'm really not very hungry. I've been travelling a lot, and what I desperately need is sleep.'

She was taken up to a charming old-fashioned room, furnished in Laura Ashley prints, with a low, raftered ceiling and a window which looked across to the church, and the lych gate, and the yew tree beyond, where a lifetime ago Saul had photographed her for the first time, and called her Primavera.

And Persephone too, she remembered. Persephone, who'd condemned herself, through one rash act, to spend half her life in the darkness of Hell.

Well, her own sentence in Hell was just beginning, and perhaps this was why she'd come back to this of all the places in the world. To start her own private and personal torment.

And also because, she realised, this would be the last place Saul would ever think of looking for her. If, indeed, he wanted to...

With a slight shiver, she drew the curtains, took off her clothes, dropping them on the floor, climbed into bed, and went almost at once into the deep sleep of sheer exhaustion.

She was eventually awakened by a light tapping on the door.

She sat up. 'Who is it?'

'It's Karen from reception. I've brought you some tea. The boss, Mrs Bennett, was getting anxious about you.'

'Oh.' Caroline stumbled out of bed, found her robe, and opened the door. 'There was really no need.'

'I told her you said you were tired.' Karen handed her the tray. 'But you've slept the clock round.'

'My goodness.' A swift glance at her watch told Caroline this was no more than the truth. She forced a smile. 'I'm sorry. I didn't realise.'

'Not to worry.' Karen gave her a friendly, if slightly speculative smile. 'Will you be eating in the dining-room tonight?'

'Yes, please.' Caroline hesitated. 'And I'll be staying on, at least until Sunday. Will that be all right?'

'It'll be fine.' Karen's smile widened into a beam. 'It's even stopped raining at last.'

It was still too early for the bar and a pre-dinner drink when Caroline came downstairs, so she decided to go for a brief stroll instead.

The clouds had vanished, and a strong evening sun was coaxing a hot, damp smell out of the wet earth and foliage. Obeying an impulse, Caroline skirted the church, and set off down the lane towards the cottage. It was as beautiful as ever, with the climbing roses coming into full bloom. But there wouldn't be any azaleas remaining down by the river. Not unless time could run back, undoing, wiping out in some way the events of the past weeks. But that, of course, was impossible. Flowers bloomed and died. Love bloomed and died. Time moved on. Time, they said, was also a great healer. But not if you were determined to keep your wound open and bleeding.

If I could have one wish in the world, she thought, it would be to walk down the path at the side of the cottage, and find the azaleas still blossoming there. Because that would mean I had the power to make a choice—to change things.

It would mean I could be back on Thyrsos with Saul, working with him each day, sleeping in his arms at night. Planning our life, our future together.

As she reached the cottage gate, she almost hesitated. Then, just in time, she saw movement in the garden, and realised that the inhabitant had returned.

She was a tall, angular, elderly woman, with strongly marked features and a mass of white hair pushed untidily under a straw hat, and she was carrying a basket and a pair of secateurs. She'd been bending over a shrub rose, and as she straightened she frowned a little, her eyes going over the girl standing by her gate, as if in some way she knew Caroline had already been an intruder on her domain, and had dared to contemplate, however briefly, a further intrusion.

She wouldn't mind, Saul had said. But this wasn't a woman who looked as if she viewed uninvited and unwanted guests with indulgence. Caroline wasn't sure what she'd expected the cottage's owner to be like, but it certainly wasn't this formidable person.

'Good evening.' The tone was resonant, with a touch of the autocrat. 'Are you lost? This lane leads only to the farm, you know.'

'I didn't realise. I'm staying at the Black Horse, and I thought I'd explore at bit—work up an appetite for dinner.' And why the hell am I explaining myself—excusing myself like this? Caroline asked in silent vexation.

'I believe it's a very popular place for tourists. Sylvia Bennett is an excellent cook.'

'Yes, well...' Under the older woman's keen, unwavering stare, Caroline found herself sorely tempted to blush and shuffle her feet. She felt like a pupil suspected of a misdemeanour in the presence of her headmistress. She tried an unconvincing smile. 'I'd better get back and sample dinner.'

'Forgive me, but are you sure you are quite well?' The other's scrutiny had sharpened, measuring her.

'I'm fine.' Caroline found she was backing away. 'Fine, really. I'm sorry I disturbed you. It's such a lovely evening.'

She had to subdue an impulse to run as she retraced her steps. She probably thinks I've escaped from somewhere, she thought wryly. And if I go on behaving like a hermit, Mrs Bennett will probably think so, too. I'm supposed to be a tourist, so I'll start acting like one.

In the morning, after breakfast, she asked the ever-helpful Karen for some details of local beauty spots, and set off with a packed lunch to look at some of them.

Over the next days, she visited gardens and toured stately homes. She tramped round potteries and craft centres, and spent an afternoon at a wildlife sanctuary.

But no amount of activity could stop her thinking, or remembering and hurting inside. Or could prevent the fact that suddenly, almost before she knew it, the following day was going to be Sunday.

She slept badly that night, and woke too early. She made herself wait almost till breakfast-time before she rang down to reception to ask if there were any Sunday papers.

'We've got an *Express* left, and an *Observer*. Oh, and a *Telegraph*. Shall I bring one up?' Karen asked.

Caroline hesitated. 'Actually the one I wanted was the *Sunday Globe*.'

'The *Globe*?' Karen's astonishment was unmistakable. 'We've never had any call for that, I'm afraid. But I could pop down to the newsagents and see if they have one,' she added doubtfully.

'Oh, please don't go to all that trouble.' Caroline bit her lip. 'I can go myself.'

'No trouble at all,' Karen said cheerfully, and rang off.

Caroline sat down on the edge of the bed. She'd had her bath. She supposed she should get dressed—go down to the dining-room. But she was reluctant to face people. In spite of Karen's assurance, someone might have seen the *Globe* already that day, and could recognise her.

If I wear dark glasses, she thought, and no make-up. And if I put my hair up...

Her reverie was interrupted by a knock at the door. She got up, tightening the sash of her robe as she moved to answer. Karen, she thought, must have flown to the newsagents and back.

She forced a smile on to her taut lips as she opened the door. She began, 'You've been quick...' then stopped on a gasp of pure terror. 'You,' she said hoarsely and began to back away. 'But it can't be. It can't be...'

'Hello, Caroline.' Saul followed her into the room and closed the door behind him. He reached into the briefcase he was carrying, and produced a copy of the *Sunday Globe* which he tossed on to the bed. 'The paper you wanted, I believe. I was able to save the receptionist a journey.'

'What are you doing here? How did you find me?'

'Oh, that was the easy part. My grandmother recognised you outside her cottage. She'd seen the photographs of you among her azaleas, and knew you were the girl I was planning to marry. But she also knew you were supposed to be in Greece with me, and she felt concerned about you—about the fact that you looked ill. So she telephoned my flat, and left a message on the machine.'

He paused. 'I didn't get it at once, unfortunately. I was with Clive, going quietly off my head. I'd found out eventually that you'd flown back to

England, and assumed there'd been some emergency. I tried your flat first, but there was no one there, so Clive seemed the next best bet. Only he was as much in the dark as I was. You'd vanished off the face of the earth, it seemed, with two rolls of very personal film.' His face was unsmiling, almost expressionless as he looked at her.

'When I mentioned the films, Marge went very quiet for a few minutes. Then she told us about your cosy tête-à-tête with Mark Clayfield at that party they gave, and how uneasy she'd always felt about it—among other things. She said she'd always felt you had another secret motive for becoming the Flawless Girl, and that she was sure now there was something desperately wrong with the entire situation.'

In a voice she didn't recognise, Caroline said, 'Marge was always—too shrewd.'

'We went back to your flat,' he went on, as if she hadn't spoken. 'And this time your flatmate was there, and she let us in. She showed us your note, and I went in your bedroom to see if you'd left any clues about your ultimate destination. And I found this.'

The torn photograph had been hastily taped back together again. She looked obscene, she thought, like a gargoyle. She swayed slightly.

'Sit down,' Saul said peremptorily. 'You're not going to faint. You're going to listen to the rest of what I have to say, and then you're going to explain why you tried to wreck the Flawless campaign.'

'Not the campaign,' she said quietly. 'Just you. I had to destroy your life as you destroyed mine.' She began to laugh. 'I had to—had to...'

The laughter was stifled with the sharp sting of Saul's fingers against her cheek.

'No fainting,' he said icily. 'And no hysterics, either. So this was a one-woman exercise to bring me down. I congratulate you. You played your part brilliantly—right to the end. Some people might say that sacrificing your virginity to add extra credibility was going over the top, but I thought it was a master-stroke. No man who'd had a woman as completely and exquisitely as I'd had you would easily believe any wrong of her.'

She put up a hand to her tingling cheek. 'Don't— please don't...'

'But I've hardly begun,' he said gently. 'I can't— compartmentalise. Not yet, anyway. Even when I knew exactly what you'd tried to do to me—to us all—I could still only remember the way your hair looked spread across my pillow. How you trembled in my arms. How you looked when you lost control.' He drew a savage breath. 'That beautiful body that only I'd seen—known.' His laugh was harsh. 'Until, of course, you handed my films to the *Globe* to develop.'

He picked up the paper, and thrust it into her hands. 'So—take a long look at the centrefold, my sweet, sexy lady. See for yourself what you've achieved. Enjoy your big moment.'

Her hands were shaking so much that the paper rattled as she opened it.

The pictures danced in front of her eyes, and she blinked in shock, trying to focus, trying to come to terms with what she saw. 'Meet shapely Donna Pride', said the caption. 'Donna, 18, from Esher, takes Pride of Place this week as our Sunday Siren.'

Donna, Caroline saw dazedly, was a busty blonde with a come-hither smile who'd had no compunction at all about what she revealed for the camera.

She said, 'I don't understand.'

'It's quite simple,' he said. 'It's called pressure. Sep Creed was in on the act by this time, and he tried to contact Clayfield to find out if our suspicions were justified, but Clayfield wouldn't take his calls. So then Sep went right to the top—to Athol Clement himself. You remember him, don't you, sweetheart? He's the guy whose hospitality you've been enjoying on Thyrsos. It turns out that the proprietor of the *Globe*, Andrew Beresford, is an old friend of his and owes him a very large favour. So your appearance in the *Globe* was summarily cancelled, and all prints and negatives were duly returned.'

Tears began to trickle down her face. 'Thank heaven,' she whispered. 'Oh, thank heaven!'

'You hypocritical little bitch.' The contempt in his voice cut her to the bone. 'You're crying because your rotten scheming hasn't worked.'

'You're wrong.' Her voice shook. 'You don't understand.'

'I've been trying to,' he came back at her grimly. 'When I found that bloody photograph and pieced it together, I could hardly believe what I was seeing—what it was suggesting. I remembered the wedding where I'd met you, and while Sep was doing his stuff I drove down there to make some enquiries, to find some motivation for this lunacy. The Foxcrofts are a well-known local family. You weren't hard to trace, now I knew who I was looking for,' he added glacially.

'I had—an illuminating talk with your parents. They told me in fascinating detail the exact lengths you'd gone to in order to alter your appearance. They seemed to take it as a personal insult. What they didn't know—and what I'm asking you now —is for goodness' sake, why?'

She pointed at the photograph. 'You see how I was.' Her voice was high and strained. 'I was a caricature—a laughing-stock. I was entitled to change the way I looked, if it could be done.'

'But you changed everything,' he said too softly. 'Even your voice is different.'

'That's because of my teeth,' she said quickly. 'I used to lisp.'

Saul came across to her, and took her by the shoulders. 'Tell me why you did this.' His voice was molten. 'Tell me why the sweet, happy child I met at that foul wedding should have put herself through this kind of ordeal. Tell me, Caroline, before I bloody well shake it out of you. Tell me why you wanted so badly to destroy me.'

His touch sang through her bones, turning them to water. Her body clenched in desire and yearning. And on the heels of that came anger.

She tore herself free and stood up. 'I'll tell you why,' she said between her teeth. 'It was because of the pathetic, childish crush I had on you, that you probably weren't even aware of. You were in the rose garden with a girl called Katie Arnold, taking pictures of her, supposedly. But you were talking about me—saying I was grotesque—an object lesson in how not to look. You said cruel, vile things. You laughed at me because I was ugly, and then—and then...'

'Yes,' Saul prompted, his eyes never leaving her face. 'What then, Caroline Foxcroft?'

Her voice thickened, broke. 'I—saw you with her. She took off her clothes—all of them. And you—you made love to her.'

There was a long silence. Saul said quietly, 'Oh, dear heaven, are you telling me I did this to you? I turned that radiant child into a monster because of something you thought you heard and saw?'

'Radiant?' she bit at him. 'How dare you say that—after the things you called me, after what you did?'

'How else would you describe yourself?' He took his wallet from his back pocket, and extracted a photograph. 'Recognise this?'

She stared down at herself. The girl she'd once been, smiling, her face shining with happiness as she played with a dog on a riverbank.

Saul said harshly, 'It's the only photograph I kept from that damned wedding. You were so sweet, so gallant and innocent, totally separate from all the bitching and manoeuvring round you. I've carried it with me ever since as a kind of talisman, to remind myself at intervals what a truly decent, lovable human being can be like.'

Her eyes blurred. She said stonily, 'You say that now. But I saw you with her. I heard you...'

'Then I'm very glad I'm not on trial, with you as a witness for the defence,' he said wearily. 'I remember that afternoon and Katie's charming striptease very vividly. I remember too that she really had her knife in you—she was clearly piqued because I preferred your company to anyone else's. I'd seen the way they all treated you, and it occurred to me that if I leapt to your defence, gave her the hard word, you'd probably suffer for it later. So I kept quiet and let her get rid of the poison inside her. At least she wasn't venting it directly on you. Probably I was wrong, but it seemed the best thing to do at the time.'

He shook his head. 'And, yes, I said you were an object lesson in how not to look, because it happened to be true. No one had ever bothered about you—paid any attention to your hair, or your skin, your posture, or the clothes you wore. It was all pretty Sister Sue, and that made me bloody angry.'

'But you wouldn't take my photograph,' she said wildly. 'You didn't want me in any of the groups.'

'Because you were so obviously the odd one out.' His voice had gentled. 'It was cruel and thoughtless of them to have asked you, knowing that your height alone made it impossible for you to fit in. And the dress was wrong for you—style, colour— everything. I didn't want to draw even more attention to the fact.'

He paused. 'I never did that book about the wedding, Caroline. I was just too disgusted with the whole scene. I simply produced some pretty-pretty conventional pictures on the day, and left it at that. However, I did wonder about you and your out-of-the-blue virus. I wondered if Katie had had a go at you, after all. In fact, I rang your house to enquire if you were better. I was going to drive over and see you, but your mother said you were resting and you couldn't be disturbed. I got the strong impression that she didn't want me around. She probably thought I was lusting after your sister. If she'd only known.'

She said, her lips moving stiffly, 'Are you pretending that you—cared about me?'

'No,' he said. 'I was certainly concerned about you—about your well-being, and what was going to happen to you. But that was as far as it went.' He gave her a straight look. 'I'd like to say that I fell in love with you, as you were then. But it wouldn't be true. All I knew was that you had an incredibly appealing personality which touched some chord in me. I wanted to protect you, and I couldn't, and that also made me angry.'

Caroline lifted her hands and pressed them to her face. 'I do remember what happened.' Her voice cracked piteously. 'I can't have got it wrong. I can't . . .'

'Think back,' Saul said quietly. 'But before you do, let's talk about what you think you saw. You watched Katie take off her bikini.'

'With your assistance.'

'I untied a couple of strings,' he said with a shrug. 'I seem to remember you invited me to do the same for you when . . .' He stopped abruptly, some of the colour draining from his face. He said, 'Of course, that whole scene was intended to be a re-run of the Katie episode, wasn't it? If I hadn't been so lost, so crazy about you, so totally turned on by what you were doing, I might have remembered.'

'Why didn't you?'

'Because it wasn't that bloody important.' Saul slammed a fist down on the chest of drawers.

'Look, Katie Arnold may have been a friend of your cousin's, but she was basically a slut and an exhibitionist. She was dying for me to photograph her nude. She'd been hinting at it from day one.' His mouth curled. 'She also presumed the sight of her body would drive me so frantic with lust that I'd have to have her there and then. But she was wrong. If I want a woman, I do my own chasing, and I made it brutally clear to her that I did not want her. She was good-looking, but she was also a spoiled, vindictive, egotistical little bitch, and I wouldn't have wished her on my worst enemy.'

He took her chin in his hand, making her look at him. 'Caroline, you may have seen the offer being made, but if you'd stayed you'd also have seen it rejected. I was no one's lover at that wedding. I was there to take pictures—and hold out a hand to a child who seemed to need a friend.'

He smoothed her hair back from her forehead. 'Now, tell me the truth. Which really mattered most to you? The comments about your appearance, or the fact that you believed I was Katie's lover?'

She said in a muffled voice, 'I ran away and was sick. I couldn't see anything, I couldn't think of anything but you—with her. I was so unhappy, I wanted to die.'

'You said it was just a childish crush,' he reminded her evenly. 'It seems to have been rather more. Crushes fade. The kind of revenge you planned needs a stronger emotion to feed on.'

She flushed dully. 'What do you want me to say? That I—loved you?'

'Only if it's true.'

She said slowly, 'Perhaps I was mistaken about that—as I was about so many things. And what does it matter, anyway, after all this time?'

'I think it matters a great deal. When we made love the other night, I asked you to marry me. You didn't give me a straight answer, which under the circumstances is understandable. But I want an answer now. Did you build this monster inside you because you loved me, and thought I'd rejected you for Katie?'

She was silent for a moment. Then she said on a sigh, 'Yes.' She released herself and moved away to sit on the edge of the bed. She stared down at the carpet. 'I was so jealous, and so angry. I—wanted to believe it was you who'd said all those things, because it made it easier to hate you—easier to blame you—for spoiling my life.' Her throat constricted painfully. 'My family didn't really care about me when I was plain—you saw that. But they liked me even less when I—changed. I was an embarrassment to them.' She gave an uneven laugh. 'I held you responsible for that, too.'

Saul knelt beside her, and took her hands in his. 'You were a hurt child hitting out in pain,' he said quietly. 'But that's behind you now, and you're a woman in every sense of the word. It isn't the past that matters, but the future.'

Her voice shook. 'But I have to go on wearing this face.'

He said patiently, 'Caroline, be honest with me. Has your life really been spoiled by your change of looks? Your family don't approve. So what? You're so lovely that you take my breath away. You have a career. You have friends who care about you. You're a success. You're the Flawless Girl.'

She shook her head. 'Not any more. Not after— all this. Clive—Sep Creed—they all know I tried to blow the campaign. They won't want to use me after this.'

He said drily, 'On the contrary, darling. You're a valuable property, and one of the reasons I'm here is to find out when you'll be ready to start work again.'

'I can't face anyone,' she said in a low voice. 'Not after what I've done.'

'After what you failed to do,' he corrected. 'The cover story is that you were naïve, and let yourself be conned by one of the *Globe*'s smooth operators. Then you got uneasy and confessed all to Sep Creed and myself, and we put a stop to it. It's as simple as that.'

'As simple as that,' she repeated, and began to cry in great, gusty sobs which clawed painfully at her throat and chest, tearing away the last remnants of bitterness and hurting. The man at her feet didn't move. He just knelt, holding her hands until the paroxysms quietened, and eventually died away.

At last, she said huskily, 'It sounds so inadequate, but I'm sorry—for everything.'

'I'm sorry too,' he said quietly. 'I'm sorry I allowed your mother to put me off that day. If I'd insisted on seeing you, perhaps it could all have been sorted out.'

'But then Carly North might never have existed.'

'Oh, I think there would have been some kind of metamorphosis, though maybe not quite such a drastic one. Carly North has cost you a great deal, in human terms particularly.' He paused. 'Anyway, it's Caroline Foxcroft that Gran is waiting to meet. She ordered me to sort everything out with you, then bring you to lunch.'

Caroline shrank. 'It's too soon. I—can't.'

He was silent for a moment, then got to his feet, shrugging. 'Then I'll have to go alone.'

He was at the door when she said, hardly breathing, 'Saul?'

He turned, his face enigmatic. 'Yes?'

She ran her tongue round her dry lips. 'You said—that you reached out a hand once to a child who needed a friend. Don't walk away—please. I—I need a friend now.'

'I need more than that,' he said. 'I need a lover, a wife, and a mother for my children. And any reaching out has to be mutual.'

She got slowly to her feet. 'You can't still want me. Not after this.'

'Listen,' he said, 'even if the *Globe* had published colour photos of you today stark naked in three dimensions, I would still love you. And I would be here with you now, helping to pick up the pieces. You are mine, and I am yours. Nothing will ever change that. And it's the woman inside you I love, not the image. Now, will you put some clothes on before I go crazy, and come and meet my grandmother?'

She began to loosen the sash of her robe. 'On the other hand, it isn't nearly lunchtime yet.'

'And guests who arrive too early are almost as bad as those who are late,' Saul agreed solemnly, watching the movement of her fingers with open fascination. 'Perhaps we should find something else to occupy us for the next hour or so.'

'It's—difficult.' The robe was loose now and, delicately, she let it slip from her shoulders and pool round her feet. 'This is a very quiet village. There isn't a great deal to do.'

'You amaze me,' Saul said, too evenly. 'I can think of any number of activities, and we don't even have to leave this room.' He reached behind him and turned the key in the lock. Then he leaned back against the panels and smiled at her. 'Say the words, lady. I need to hear them from you.'

She said quietly and clearly, 'I love you. I think always have, and I know I always will. And I'll marry you whenever you want me to.'

He came to her then, lifting her against his heart.

He said softly, 'My sweet—my flawless love.' And his mouth sought hers in tenderness and promise.

Harlequin Presents

Coming Next Month

#1287 BELONGING Sally Cook
Mandy always knew she was adopted, but having grown up so different from her adoptive parents, she decides to trace her real mother. While her search is successful, she finds the attractive Grant Livingstone is highly suspicious of her motives.

#1288 THE ULTIMATE CHOICE Emma Darcy
According to Kelly, the new owner of Marian Park is an arrogant swine who betrayed her grandfather and who wants to ruin Kelly's show-jumping career. Determined not to be stopped, she confronts Justin St. John, with all guns blazing....

#1289 TAKING CHANCES Vanessa Grant
It seems an odd request even for Misty's detective agency. Why does Zeb Turner want her to kidnap him? Finding out, Misty lands herself with more than she'd bargained for—maybe even more than she can cope with!

#1290 RUNAWAY WIFE Charlotte Lamb
Francesca has everything, so it seems—Oliver, her handsome, successful husband; a healthy son; and a lovely home. She believes she's merely a symbol of his success to Oliver and needs—and wants—far more than that from life.

#1291 THE SEDUCTION OF SARA Joanna Mansell
Sara isn't too pleased to have Lucas Farraday following her around Peru. She thinks he's just a penniless drifter. Gradually she relaxes and gets used to his presence and his help. And that's when Lucas makes his next move....

#1292 RECKLESS HEART Kate Proctor
Ever since Sian McAllister's new boss, Nicholas Sinclair, had jumped to the wrong conclusions about her, life has been difficult. And the situation becomes impossible when Sian realizes that despite their strong disagreements, she's falling in love with him.

#1293 GENTLE DECEPTION Frances Roding
Rosy's love for her married cousin, Elliott, is entirely platonic, but not everyone sees it that way. To prove them wrong, Rosy has to find herself a man. Callum Blake is perfectly willing to be her pretend lover—yet what if pretence becomes reality?

#1294 DESIGNED WITH LOVE Kathryn Ross
Drew Sheldon is Amanda's ex-fiancé—and when her father sells the family firm to him, Amanda has a problem. She needs her job, but can she live with the power Drew now holds over her when she has an idea he really might want revenge?

Available in August wherever paperback books are sold, or through Harlequin Reader Service:

In the U.S.
901 Fuhrmann Blvd.
P.O. Box 1397
Buffalo, N.Y. 14240-1397

In Canada
P.O. Box 603
Fort Erie, Ontario
L2A 5X3

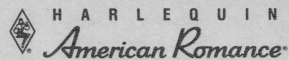

Harlequin Superromance

A powerful restaurant conglomerate that draws the best and brightest to its executive ranks. Now almost eighty years old, Vanessa Hamilton, the founder of Hamilton House, must choose a successor.
Who will it be?

Matt Logan: He's always been the company man, the quintessential team player. But tragedy in his daughter's life and a passionate love affair made him make some hard choices....

Paula Steele: Thoroughly accomplished, with a sharp mind, perfect breeding and looks to die for, Paula thrives on challenges and wants to have it all...
but is this right for her?

Grady O'Connor: Working for Hamilton House was his salvation after Vietnam. The war had messed him up but good and had killed his storybook marriage. He's been given a second chance—only he doesn't know what the hell he's supposed to do with it....

Harlequin Superromance invites you to enjoy Barbara Kaye's dramatic and emotionally resonant miniseries about mature men and women making life-changing decisions. Don't miss:

- CHOICE OF A LIFETIME—a July 1990 release.
- CHALLENGE OF A LIFETIME
  —a December 1990 release.
- CHANCE OF A LIFETIME—an April 1991 release.